Spiky passed he[...] obliged him by reading aloud: "LARGE UNIDENTIFIED FLYING OBJECT REPORTED OVER THE SEA. A large object, shaped like a diamond, was reported last night to be circling high over the sea. Several observers phoned the police, and a constable with binoculars confirmed that he could see what he described as a triangular object in the sky, but it immediately rose to a great height and vanished. The policeman in question said he had never seen such an object before, and denied that there was any possibility that it could have been a plane or a balloon.''

'So what?' was Anna's comment when she had finished reading, 'What's that to do with my meteorites?'

Also in Beaver by Philip Curtis
Mr Browser meets the Burrowers

MR BROWSER
AND THE
MINI-METEORITES

Philip Curtis

Illustrated by Tony Ross

Beaver Books

A Beaver Book

Published by Arrow Books Limited
62-65 Chandos Place, London WC2N 4NW

An imprint of Century Hutchinson Ltd

London Melbourne Sydney Auckland
Johannesburg and agencies throughout
the world

First published by Andersen Press, London, 1983
Beaver edition 1986

Printed and bound in Great Britain by
Anchor Brendon Limited, Tiptree, Essex

ISBN 0 09 943670 1

Contents

1

The First of the Mini-Meteorites

'I think that Mondays ought to be added to the weekend, especially in summer,' said Spiky Jackson to his friend Michael Fairlie as they walked up the path to the school playground one Monday morning. Michael was about to agree, when peace was shattered by the roar of a motor-bike arriving in the school car park.

The boys watched as Mr Caracco, the new

teacher of Class 7, came to a halt and started to dismount. This wasn't too easy, because Mr Caracco had a guitar and a rucksack strapped to his back, which threatened his balance as he almost fell off the bike. Mr Caracco was an athletic young man, and he managed the manoeuvre successfully. He went into Chivvy Chase School by the kitchen door, no doubt hoping for a cup of tea from the cook.

'Sometimes,' said Spiky thoughtfully, 'I wish I could be in Class 7.'

'Why?' asked Michael.

'Because they're always going out to different places and looking in ponds for newts and acting plays – and he plays the guitar for their music lessons – '

'And he often gets mad with them, and keeps them in after school,' put in Michael. 'Old Browser doesn't do that more than about once a term, and then it's only for five minutes.'

Spiky considered this, then came to the point that was troubling him most.

'They're going out all day to the beach on Friday,' he grumbled. 'We never do that sort of thing. Old Browser's doing Australia this term, and the nearest you can come to possums and wombats and koalas is to see them stuffed at the Commonwealth Institute.'

8

'Suppose you're right,' admitted Michael, who had just seen two more of his friends in the playground. Spiky's grumbles, he thought, weren't going to change anything.

'Race you to the playground!' he challenged Spiky, and in a flash the race was on.

At the same time as Spiky was voicing his complaints, something was being done about the matter of the visit to the beach. Mr Browser, while walking up the stairs to Classroom 8, met the Headmaster on the way down.

'Morning, George,' Mr Sage greeted him. In earlier years Mr Browser would have welcomed this friendly greeting on a Monday morning as a sign that Mr Sage was in a contented frame of mind, but now he wondered what it was the Headmaster wanted of him.

'Morning, Mr Sage,' he replied cautiously.

'I hope you had a pleasant weekend,' went on Mr Sage. 'By the way, has your class been on a visit this term?'

'Not yet,' replied Mr Browser. 'Maybe we'll be going to the Commonwealth Institute later on –'

'I was wondering,' cut in the Headmaster, 'if you'd like your class to go with Mr Caracco's to the beach next Friday. The coach firm can only provide a fifty-seater, and it needs another class to go in order to cut the cost. It would make a pleasant day

9

if the weather holds.'

Mr Browser had his doubts, but he put them diplomatically.

'We're not studying the sea this term,' he explained. 'We're starting on a topic about Australia – '

'Again?' said Mr Sage. 'I should think you could squeeze in a little local nature study. Make the visit first, let them bring back a few finds from the beach, and then talk about them. It would help Mr Caracco no end.'

So Mr Browser was not surprised to find himself, on the following Friday morning, bringing up the rear as Mr Caracco led the two classes into the coach for the half hour's journey to the beach. Mr Caracco's class were all excellently equipped for the visit, many of them carrying shrimping nets and jars and tins into which to put their finds. Mr Browser's children were chiefly equipped with their packed lunches, but they appeared to be looking forward to the outing with just as much pleasure.

The journey to the seaside passed with only one incident – when a child in Mr Caracco's class poked Anna Cardwell in the eye with the end of the cane of his shrimping net. Mr Caracco jumped up and shouted at the boy concerned, and Mr Browser had to calm the situation down by pointing out that Anna had been secretly stuffing the boy's net with old sweet papers, and so maybe deserved her fate.

When they arrived Mr Caracco gave out a list of warnings about what they were not to do, and threatened that if they didn't behave he would take them back to school at once. Mr Browser seconded this, but as the coach driver drove off immediately he had unloaded the children, it was difficult to see how Mr Caracco was going to get them back to school, unless he made them walk ten miles. Then a section of the beach between two groynes was invaded, and a couple of old age pensioners there to enjoy a quiet snooze woke up in disgust at the state to which the world had come.

Socks and shoes were pulled off, stones were thrown at an old tin can, and Mr Browser settled down on the sand hoping that no one would lose himself.

'The tide's out!' shouted Spiky Jackson, who would have liked to go swimming.

'I know. I arranged it that way,' said Mr Caracco. Stripped to the waist and in a pair of shorts, he was ready to begin the closest inspection the shore had ever known.

'Don't forget – you're not to go beyond the first motor-boat lying out there on the mud,' he ordered them. 'Those with shrimping nets, take one person with a jar and see what you can find in the pools. The rest look for shells and any unusual stones or

11

seaweeds. Leave your lunches here with Mr Browser – and away we go!'

'Shall we do the same, Mr Browser?' asked Anna.

'Of course. And if you find anything interesting, bring it to me.'

But it was unlikely that anyone would do that at once, because in order to reach the pools and the mud a long stretch of stony beach had to be crossed. Mr Caracco covered this in bare feet as though he were walking on an Indian carpet, but Anna and some others who were also barefooted let out shrieks as they picked their way over the pebbles.

It seems as though Nature's creatures are prepared these days for young visitors, and make themselves as scarce as possible. Crabs buried themselves in the mud, and shrimps hid under stones. The searchers began to move further away from the beach, and Mr Caracco kept on urging them to be patient and not to disturb the creatures by their movements. Spiky Jackson, Michael Fairlie and Anna, not being so obliged to return with a good harvest of objects for study, wandered further and further out until the water of a little creek was playing about their ankles. They paddled through the stream and reached the motor-boat, tilted over in the mud, which Mr Caracco had warned them was to be the limit of their explorations. Anna hugged the side of the boat and crept around it. On

12

the other side of it was another creek, and then a beautiful brown stretch of hard sand, extending for fifty metres or so. The temptation of that sand was too great for Anna.

'Race you across that sandbank,' she called to Spiky. 'It must be great out there. We can be there and back in a few minutes. Look – Caracco's showing a crab to some of his kids. Bet you I can beat you there and back!'

When Spiky and Michael peered round the stern of the boat, Anna was already wading across the little stream. The sight of the golden brown sand was too much for the boys to resist, and they chased after her, splashing water into each other's faces as they ran through the water and up on the sand. Anna ran well and led them as far as the next creek, which was larger and wider, but on the way back the boys caught up with her, and they all three suddenly stopped, out of breath, and lay down on the firm sand.

'We'd better not stay here long,' said Michael. 'Mr Caracco may find us –'

'I don't care what "Crackers" says,' declared Anna. 'We're in Mr Browser's class.'

'That makes no difference,' Michael began to argue. 'We'd better be going –'

'Just a moment!' Spiky Jackson interrupted him urgently. One of his fingers was deep in the sand,

and he was moving it around as if to free something.

'There's some sort of shell under here,' he told them. 'It feels sharp at the top.'

'Come on, we'd better hurry,' said Michael, standing up and pulling Anna to her feet.

'It's not a shell,' went on Spiky, now digging in the sand with both hands. 'Look! It's a kind of stone.'

Anna gave the stone a quick inspection.

'It's like two pyramids stuck together,' she said. 'A sort of diamond shape. Show it to Mr Browser when we get back.'

'Hurry up – oh, it's too late,' said Michael. 'It's Caracco – he's seen us!'

'Come back at once, you three!' shouted Mr Caracco, appearing at the side of the boat. 'Move yourselves, or I'll report you to Mr Browser and Mr Sage!'

'Quick, Spiky!' cried Anna, and started to run. 'Bring that stone thing with you.'

Spiky was still grovelling in the sand, sure he had felt something else hard near his discovered stone. He was right. Soon he had clawed out another stone. He put it on the sand alongside the first one and compared them. As far as he could see, they were identical in shape and appearance. As Anna had put it, each one was formed as though two pyramids had been stuck together, base to base – only there was no join. They were made of a dull, grey, metallic substance.

'Jackson! Move yourself, or I'll move you!' threatened Mr Caracco. Spiky sprang to his feet and put the two objects in his pocket. Then, on second thoughts he took one of them out again and ran with it in his hand across the sand and back to the boat.

'Simon Jackson, why do you have to break the rules?' Mr Caracco greeted him.

'Sorry, Mr Caracco, we forgot,' Spiky excused himself. 'Look what I've found, Mr Caracco. Is it a stone? It's not a shell.'

Mr Caracco looked rather angrily at the object. He had not been teaching for very long, and he believed that a teacher should know everything. He had never seen an object like the one Spiky was holding in any of the books on the seashore which he had studied. He frowned at it, unwilling to admit that he didn't know.

'Just a stone, I suppose. Better show it to Mr Browser. We're all going back to the beach to have lunch. You'd better hop it!'

Spiky hopped it, trying to catch up with Anna and Michael, who had already been ordered back to the beach. When they had all safely reached the shore, Mr Caracco ran out in the other direction, stripped to a pair of swimming trunks and enjoyed a

brief swim in the creek. When he came back the party was busy eating sandwiches, and Mr Browser was holding the funny object Spiky had found and inspecting it from all angles.

'I've never seen anything like this before,' said Mr Browser to Mr Caracco. 'Seems kind of metallic, and it's perfectly formed. A beautiful shape.'

Now that Mr Browser had confessed ignorance, Mr Caracco found it easier to do so himself.

'Beats me,' he confessed. 'That young rogue found it out on the sandbank beyond the boat.'

'Was it lying on the sand, Simon?' asked Mr Browser.

'No, in it,' replied Spiky. 'I felt that the sand was

17

soft in one spot, and I pushed my fingers into it, and the middle one struck the point of this stone.'

'Curious,' mumbled Mr Browser. 'There was a report that somebody saw what he thought was a shower of meteorites falling out at sea a few nights ago, but not much was made of it. This looks the right sort of material for a meteorite – but it's much too precisely shaped. No, it beats me, Simon. You'd better bring it into school and we'll see if Mr Sage or someone else can throw any light on it.'

'Yes, Mr Browser.'

Spiky put the object back in his left pocket, so that it didn't rattle against its secret twin in his right pocket. Then he ate the rest of his lunch and enjoyed the game of cricket Mr Caracco organised in the afternoon. In the coach on the way home Mr Browser nearly fell asleep, but Mr Caracco produced his guitar and led the passengers in some community singing all the way back to school. The coach driver drove as fast as he could, and the crabs and the shrimps and winkles and cockles were all under water, so they weren't disturbed at all.

'I suppose I ought to join in the singing,' thought Mr Browser drowsily, but sat back and quietly tried to puzzle out exactly what the curious object Spiky had shown him could be. He was quite sure that Mr Sage would be no more able to explain it than he could himself.

2

An Object Comes to Life

When the coach arrived back at Chivvy Chase the bell for the end of school had already been rung. Everyone was in a hurry to go home, and Mr Sage was nowhere to be found. So Spiky kept his two finds in his pockets and only examined them closely in his bedroom that evening.

They were both perfectly shaped and as smooth as pebbles, with a colour resembling that of iron filings. He found his old magnet, and when he approached them with it the objects slid across the dressing table towards it and attached themselves firmly, so that he had to use strength to pull them away.

When he went to the bathroom and put them in water, they sank. When he took them out, the water slipped away from them in droplets and left them dry. When he tried scraping one of them with a penknife, it made no effect at all, not even leaving a mark. Then he stood on the bed and dropped them on the floor, and when that brought no result he could think of no further experiments. He put one of them under his pillow and took the other downstairs to show to his father, who had just come in from work. But Spiky's dad was only interested in things he knew about and understood. He hardly gave the object a second's thought.

'Probably part of some kid's building set,' was his verdict, and Spiky put the shape in his pocket and decided to leave further investigation until the next Monday morning; he had great faith that if Mr Browser couldn't solve the mystery, the Headmaster would certainly be able to do so.

On Monday morning Mr Sage spent a pleasant half hour amongst the crabs and shrimps and seaweeds so expertly collected by Mr Caracco's class. Then he visited Class 8, whose smaller exhibition was on show on a table just inside the door.

'I hope the visit was worthwhile, Mr Browser,' said Mr Sage doubtfully.

'I'm sure it was,' replied Mr Browser cheerfully. 'We all enjoyed it very much.'

That wasn't quite what Mr Sage had meant, and he went on to question the children closely about what they had found.

'Nothing very unusual, then,' he concluded.

'For the most part, no,' agreed Mr Browser. 'But we'd be very pleased if you could tell us about an object Simon Jackson found, Mr Sage. I don't think he's put it out on display.'

'What's that?' asked Mr Sage, evidently believing that if the object were not worth displaying it couldn't be of much importance.

'I have it on my desk, Mr Sage,' said Spiky, and passed the object across to the Headmaster.

Mr Sage was a most thorough man, and he honoured Spiky's find with a far longer inspection than anyone else had afforded it. He took it to the window and held it up to the light, tapped it against a desk and then squeezed it in his hand. But his attempts to gain evidence about it were no more successful than Spiky's, and when he realised he couldn't give a name to the thing he began to lose interest and found an excuse for his lost enthusiasm.

'This has a perfect geometrical shape,' he admit-

ted, giving it back to Spiky, 'but I doubt if it has any special connection with the sea or the beach. No doubt it's some oddity which has dropped out of someone's pocket and become buried in the sand. Part of a game, perhaps.'

'Please sir!' called out Anna.

'Yes, Anna?'

'Perhaps it could have dropped from the sky, Mr Sage. Suppose it was one of those meteorites that they talked about in the paper the other day – you know, the ones that were seen like a shower of sparks in the sky!'

Mr Sage looked solemn. He didn't like Anna suggesting that he knew something, and her enthusiasm was making her too free and easy in the way she spoke to him.

'They didn't talk about it in the paper, Anna,' he said. 'They wrote about it.'

Anna shrugged her shoulders.

'Yes, I do know about the meteorites,' he went on. 'But if you read the report carefully, you will have seen that it was thought that the meteorites must have burnt themselves out before they reached the earth.'

'But suppose they didn't!' whispered Selwyn Jordan.

Mr Sage pretended not to hear him. 'Also,' he declared, 'if any small pieces did manage to reach the ground, they would show signs of burning and would certainly not be as exactly shaped as this is. No, Anna, I'm afraid your theory is not on the mark. Here you are, Simon. I look forward to seeing some work about shells and sea creatures, Mr Browser.'

Mr Sage walked out.

'He didn't know what it is,' muttered Spiky, and put the mysterious object back in his pocket. There it remained until late in the afternoon, when the sun was shining through the west facing windows and Mr Browser, with the help of some textbooks, was explaining how difficult life could be for Australian farmers.

Twenty minutes to go. Spiky took out his mysterious find once more and fingered it curiously. The sun shone upon it, and the surface glinted as it reflected the light. Spiky recalled the magnifying glass inside his desk – last used to flash patches of light on the ceiling. Mr Browser had quickly killed off this activity by threatening to take the glass away. Now Spiky edged it out of the desk and held it between the sun and the object, so that the rays were centred on one of the pointed ends. Idly he held the glass in the same position for a whole minute, and he calculated that the heat he was generating would have been enough to set a piece of paper smouldering.

The object gave the impression that it was as resistant to heat as it had been to water, to squeezing and to tapping. What an uninteresting, useless object, Spiky was thinking; perhaps it would be possible to swop it for a few marbles or a model car, if he were lucky. As he stared critically at it, he thought it trembled. Ridiculous, he told himself – and then the object began to hiss. First only Spiky heard the hissing, then Michael and Selwyn, who were sitting near him, were attracted by the sound. Next Anna, two desks away, turned round out of curiosity.

'What do you want, Spiky?' asked Michael in a whisper, thinking that Spiky was making the hissing noise himself. For answer Spiky pointed to his desk, on which the mystery object, as if overcome by its own power, was beginning to spin round as it hissed even louder.

'Simon! Stop that noise, and pay attention!' called out Mr Browser.

'It's not me, Mr Browser!' pleaded Spiky. By now a dozen children were watching the spinning object, and Mr Browser stood up and came towards Spiky's desk.

Suddenly, with a huge hiss, like that made by a giant balloon when it suddenly loses air, the shape spun off Spiky's desk and whipped across the floor. The hissing became so intense that many of the class

put their hands over their ears – and Mr Browser stood still in his tracks. Still the hissing grew, until it reached its climax in a dull explosion.

Hands were taken from ears, and the class began to relax – but then came the strangest sensation of all, experienced by everyone but only related later on.

'I felt as though a spider's web had come up from the floor and brushed past my face,' was Anna's description.

'A kind of thin film touched my hands and face,' said Michael.

'It was as though a puff of air pushed past me,' explained Selwyn.

At the time, Mr Browser pushed his thinning hair back with his hand, certain that something had touched it in passing.

'Give me that thing,' he ordered Selwyn, who was carefully inspecting the object that seemed to have caused all the trouble. Gingerly Selwyn picked it up and passed it to Mr Browser, who studied it closely.

'It doesn't seem to have changed,' he observed, and handed it back to Spiky. 'Are you sure no one has a balloon hidden away?' he demanded of the class.

'No, Mr Browser – honest, it was that thing of Spiky's – that mini-meteorite,' declared Anna, and amid laughter Mr Browser shook his head and urged them all to return to work for the last five minutes of the afternoon. They obeyed extremely promptly, but he didn't remark on this – children still remained capable of surprising him even after all his years in the classroom. He did, however, feel particularly pleased with himself and his work at the end of the afternoon, and congratulated the children on their behaviour as they quietly left the room. They went out with contented, smiling faces, and Mr Browser himself left happily for home some five minutes later. In the corridor downstairs he met Mr Sage.

'Well, George, had a good day?' asked the Headmaster jovially. 'It was very good of you to take your class with Mr Caracco's to the beach on Friday.'

'No trouble, Mr Sage, we all enjoyed it,' replied Mr Browser.

'Have a good evening, then,' went on the Headmaster. 'Take care – we don't want teachers like you overdoing it. Make sure you relax.'

'Thank you, Mr Sage.'

Only when he was on the road in his car did Mr Browser reflect that he'd never heard Mr Sage speak like that before. He really seemed to mean his kind words.

And only when he was on the road in his car did Mr Sage pause to wonder why he had spoken like that to old Browser. He would have been even more surprised had he known what was going on inside his school after he had left. Mr Caracco, who had kept six of his children behind because they had annoyed him earlier in the day, had intended to set them some extra maths. to punish them. When the bell for the end of school rang, he was suddenly filled with a desire to let them go.

'I won't keep you tonight,' he announced. 'Maybe I've been a little harsh on you. Off you go, now.'

Normally this instruction would have been instantly acted upon – but the wrongdoers sat there with expressions verging on disappointment.

'We're sorry we misbehaved,' said one of them. 'We really ought to pay for it.'

'That's right,' agreed one or two more.

'Well,' said Mr Caracco, 'I'm sure that's very decent of you. Now, what can we do? I know – I'll fetch my guitar and we'll have a little singing together before we go.'

So they did, and they only agreed to go home to please the caretaker, Mr Watchett, and because their mums might be growing worried, according to Mr Caracco.

Only when he was speeding home on his motor-bike did Mr Caracco think to question why he had acted in this way, and why the children had been so unusually helpful and appreciative. Even the care-

taker had declared that he wouldn't mind Mr
Caracco staying in his room as long as he liked.

It was a happy ending to the day, but like Mr
Browser and Mr Sage, Mr Caracco faintly suspected that something odd had happened at Chivvy
Chase; but he supposed that next morning he would
find everything as normal as usual.

3

The Happiest School in the Land

Anna Cardwell was one of the first to pass the school gate the next morning, and she was in none too happy a mood. It was to be a day without a swimming lesson or a T. V. programme or a games period – and it was quite likely that Mr Browser would pounce and produce one of those printed tests which he delighted in setting the class from time to time. Anna scowled at the thought – and then her expression changed.

It seemed to her that she had just passed through an invisible spider's web – the sensation was just the same as that she had experienced on the previous afternoon. She walked on, and realised that now she was looking forward to the day and all its activities with pleasure – even the test would be bearable.

Back at the gate, Spiky Jackson called out to her. 'Anna! Have a look at this!' He was waving a newspaper at her. Anna turned and ran back – and at the same point on the path she had that uncanny feeling of breaking through something.

'Anna – remember what you said about meteorites the other day?'

'Yes – it was nonsense, old Sage said!'

'Maybe it wasn't, Anna. I've found the report in the paper. Read this!'

Spiky passed her the newspaper, and Anna obliged him by reading aloud: ' "LARGE UNIDENTIFIED FLYING OBJECT REPORTED OVER THE SEA. A large object, shaped like a diamond, was reported last night to be circling high over the sea. Several observers phoned the police, and a constable with binoculars confirmed that he could see what he described as a triangular object in the sky, but it immediately rose to a great height and vanished. The policeman in question said he had never seen such an object before, and denied that there was any possibility that it could have been a plane or a balloon." '

'So what?' was Anna's comment when she had finished reading. 'What's that to do with my meteorites?'

'Only,' said Spiky, 'the shape of this large object seems to be the same as that of my little ones. And suppose, instead of the meteorites mentioned in the other report, the shower of sparks was really a lot of these little objects falling into the sea?'

'Suppose,' said Anna, 'they didn't fall from the sky, but were shot from the bigger object?'

'You've hit it,' said Spiky, thinking that Anna was a girl to be admired.

'But I can't believe it's true,' went on Anna. 'Why should a useless object like yours be shot down specially to earth?'

'Maybe it's not useless,' said Spiky.

'It can't do anything,' argued Anna.

'Yes it can –'

'Well, if you call hissing and spinning round doing something useful, then I suppose it does,' said Anna condescendingly. 'I don't see much point in it myself.'

Spiky was ready to defend his mysterious possessions, and was all set to annoy Anna by pulling her satchel from her shoulder, when the pair of them passed through the invisible film, and Spiky immediately withdrew his grabbing hand.

'Sorry, Anna,' he said. 'It's not worth worrying about.'

'It's a lovely idea, Spiky,' said Anna sweetly. 'Maybe we'll find out one day that there is some purpose in that thing.'

They reached the playground and mingled with other members of Class 8, who were talking amiably together or playing peaceful games. The playground at Chivvy Chase was often a quiet place before school in the morning, and no one became suspicious because there were no fights or squabbles or tears. Even children who fell over picked themselves up cheerfully and made no complaint.

The teachers on duty wondered a little at the orderly, quiet way in which the children happily filed into school – but they were in contented mood themselves, and decided that the pleasant weather must be the reason for the children's unusually good behaviour. But by the time the morning assembly came, some of the staff, including Mr Browser and Mr Caracco, became suspicious.

The children sat quietly waiting for Mr Sage, and Miss Toms didn't have to say a word to a single child, nor did she have to raise her eyebrows, which she often did as a preliminary warning to fidgets. Mr Sage came in, and he smiled at everybody in the hall.

'Thank you, Miss Toms,' he said. 'It's marvellous to see such an attentive group of children. I feel really proud of Chivvy Chase School.'

The children smiled back, and Mr Browser couldn't help wondering if the older children really meant their smiles and good behaviour – but Spiky and Michael and Anna and the rest were sitting there with straight backs, as good as gold. And so they remained throughout the short service conducted by Mr Sage. At the end of the service Mr Sage often said a few words, perhaps warning against the dropping of litter or banning all running in the school corridors – but today he had nothing but praise for the school.

'It's a real pleasure to work with such a hard working, well behaved group of children,' he declared. 'I won't delay you any longer, because I'm sure you'll be wanting to get down to some work.'

'We do, Mr Sage, we do!' called out some of the youngest children at the front, and from the back came Lee Franks' loud voice.

'Three cheers for Mr Sage!' he shouted, and the whole school joined in – and after the three cheers returned to satisfied silence.

Now at the end of the school year, or when they are retiring at the end of their careers, headmasters may expect three cheers, but on an ordinary school day – never! No wonder Mr Browser looked amazed, and Miss Toms suspected that some mischief was afoot. But all was well – the happy pupils hurried off to their various classrooms in silent and expectant lines.

'That was very nice of you, Lee,' said Mr Caracco to the boy who was often his most awkward pupil. 'I'm sure Mr Sage will appreciate those three cheers a great deal.'

Mr Caracco had been teaching for such a short time that he didn't fully realise how remarkable it was to give three cheers in the middle of the term; all he knew was that he was feeling extremely happy at the prospect of teaching his class long division of number. His class seemed equally keen to be taught.

In Mr Browser's classroom, too, the atmosphere was one of well-being, harmony and helpfulness. Children who couldn't quite understand their maths. were extremely upset about it, even those like Spiky, who usually found it easy to put a brave face on when in difficulty.

'Could you give us some homework, Mr Browser, so that we can make quite sure we've understood everything?' asked Anna.

'But children,' Mr Browser heard himself saying, 'your spare time is precious. You've worked so hard, I'm sure you won't need homework.'

'Oh, we don't mind!' called out several of the class, and the rest showed their approval of the idea on their faces.

At playtime Mr Browser let them our promptly and hurried to the staffroom for his coffee. Mr Caracco came in immediately after him.

'Wonderful morning I've had,' declared Mr Caracco. 'I've never enjoyed teaching so much! They lapped up long division, so I gave them a song on my guitar.'

'I've had a good morning too,' admitted Mr Browser, and when the other teachers came in and revealed that their children had behaved like angels as well, he scratched his head and became a little suspicious. Such universal happiness was unusual for any school, let alone Chivvy Chase. It was even more disturbing when Mr Sage put his head round the door to make an announcement.

'We'll give them an extra ten minutes' play,' he said. 'They've deserved it, don't you think?'

'Of course,' the majority of the staff agreed at once – and Mr Browser could see that they really meant it. Whatever was going on at Chivvy Chase? He sat in the corner and allowed the happy conversation to flow all around him, and couldn't find any explanation for his own unease – nor did he try very hard, for he was in such a happy state of mind himself.

Out in the playground all was as happy and harmonious as in the staffroom. Nobody squabbled, and if the boys' games of football interfered with the girls who were skipping, the boys at once apologised and the girls said it didn't matter at all.

Spiky Jackson approached the cheer leader, a stocky boy called Lee Franks, who wore his hair close cropped. Lee was hanging about by the railings looking as near to discontented as anyone amongst the happy band.

'Say, Lee, that was a great idea of yours, calling for three cheers for old Sage,' said Spiky. 'Yet you're not looking very happy.'

'No, I'm not,' admitted Lee. 'I think I ought to be happy, but something's worrying me.'

'What?' asked Spiky sympathetically. 'Tell me

about it.'

'It's my dad,' he confessed. 'He told me this morning that he was coming up to school to complain about Mr Caracco.'

'Complain? Why?'

'He says he doesn't make us work. Says he's always playing the guitar and taking us out on visits. My dad said' – and Lee hesitated at the prospect – 'he's going to have a big bust-up with old Sage and with Crackers too. I'm afraid of what he'll do. He's like a mad bull, my dad is, when his temper's up!'

'I know!' said Spiky feelingly, for he had been on the wrong end of Mr Franks' boot once for breaking one of his greenhouse windows. 'Caracco's not a bad teacher, though, is he? I wouldn't mind being in your class.'

'Caracco's all right,' said Lee. 'Gets a bit excited when we annoy him, and keeps us in too often. Sometimes I'd rather be with old Browser – but Crackers means well. But look, Spiky! There's my dad!'

The worry lines on Lee's face deepened, and Spiky saw why. Along the pavement by the railings Mr Joe Franks was striding, fierce determination all over his face. He was a bull-necked, solid man who had once been a professional footballer. 'Nobody,' he had told Lee often, 'can call himself a proper professional until he's broken his nose at least three times.' Joe Franks had broken his nose five times and it showed in his appearance.

'Oh dear,' groaned Lee, 'I hope there won't be a punch-up. Everybody's feeling so happy, and my dad has to come and spoil it.'

'Don't worry,' Spiky tried to console him. 'With a bit of luck he won't get to see Caracco. Old Sage will take him to his room.'

'I'm afraid of that, too,' admitted Lee. 'My dad says old Sage is just as much to blame.'

They watched as Franks senior strode up the path and into the school. Joe Franks was indeed in a mood for action when he passed the school gate. He hated these 'new-fangled ideas', as he put it, and he was ready for trouble as he came into the school grounds. The outlook for Mr Sage and Mr Caracco was grim as he came up the path. With a critical grunt he pushed aside what he thought was a cobweb, and when he reached the school door he stopped and scratched his head before entering.

Miss Copewell, the vigilant secretary, had seen him striding past the office window, and she appeared at the door just at the right moment.

'Morning, Mr Franks,' she said brightly. 'Lovely day, isn't it!'

'Yes,' said Joe.

'Did you want to see Mr Sage?'

'Er – yes please, if he's not too busy.'

'Is it about anything special?'

Miss Copewell was aware that Joe could be as troublesome as his son, and wanted to warn Mr Sage if possible. But Joe, who had meant to be so blunt, hesitated and was at first lost for words. Then he stammered: 'I've come to – to see about my boy's progress –'

'Do come in, Mr Franks,' said Miss Copewell. 'I'm sure Mr Sage will be delighted to see you.'

'Mr Franks,' she announced to Mr Sage, 'come to see about little Lee's progress.'

'Ah – welcome, Mr Franks,' Mr Sage greeted him. 'You couldn't have come on a better morning. I am most pleased with Lee. Why, he even led the

40

school in three cheers for me this morning in assembly.'

'Did he really?' said Joe, gawping at Mr Sage. 'Well, I've always said Lee's a good lad.'

'Yes, and he has a good teacher, too,' went on Mr Sage happily. 'He's making great strides in Mr Caracco's class.'

'Indeed?'

'Yes, surely. Let's go and have a look at the class now, Mr Franks. I'm sure a visit will prove my point.'

'Well – er – I don't want to be a nuisance,' said Joe humbly.

'Far from it,' declared Mr Sage. 'We love to see parents at Chivvy Chase. It's a happy school, and I must say, it's never been happier than today.'

They went upstairs and passed Mr Browser's room, where the children were happily making clay models of kangaroos, emus and the duck-billed platypus. As they approached Mr Caracco's room, the sound of the guitar could be heard. Mr Caracco was teaching English by telling a story in song, which the children were to write out afterwards in their own words. It did occur to Mr Joe Franks that the guitar was one of the main reasons for his visit and his anger – but somehow it didn't seem to matter any more. Mr Sage opened the classroom door and encouraged Mr Franks inside, thereby

41

causing Lee Franks to turn pale and clutch the edges of his chair in fear of what might be about to happen. Mr Caracco stopped playing and singing.

'No, no, please go on,' begged Mr Sage. 'We don't want to interrupt, do we, Mr Franks?'

'No, of course not,' muttered Joe. They listened for a while, and then crept out again.

'The modern approach,' said Mr Sage. 'Did you notice how happily the children were listening?'

'You couldn't miss it,' said Joe, and expressed himself completely satisfied, indeed delighted, with all that was going on at Chivvy Chase School. Miss Copewell gave him a cup of tea, and he parted from Mr Sage with a hearty handshake.

Spiky Jackson, who happened to be outside knocking Mr Browser's blackboard duster free of chalk on the edge of the playground, saw Lee's father and Mr Sage shaking hands, and watched Joe Franks stroll contentedly down the path to the gate.

Suddenly, halfway down, Joe stopped, passed his hand over his face and turned back to look at the school. As he did so, another man was walking up the path. This was Mr Jolyon Morten, the Inspector, making one of his occasional visits to Chivvy Chase. Mr Morten had eaten too many oysters the night before, and now had a little indigestion, so he, like Joe, wanted to find fault with Chivvy Chase

School – only in a much more polite way.

'They've done me again!' said Joe out loud, and shook his fist at the school.

'I beg your pardon?' asked Mr Morten.

'Done me!' repeated Joe, puzzled. 'Made me feel happy when I wasn't! I've a good mind to –'

'Yes?'

'Oh, never mind,' said Joe, and skulked off home to grumble at Mrs Franks for one reason or another.

Mr Jolyon Morten shook his head as he passed through the invisible film, and when Spiky opened the door for him the Inspector was already in the best mood he'd been in since he left his favourite school days before.

'Good boy,' he said to Spiky. 'It's a pleasure to meet with such polite children as you.'

And for the rest of the morning he had nothing but praise for Mr Sage and Chivvy Chase School. Only when he returned to his car, passing through that strange sensation on the path in order to do so, did he pause to think about what had happened to him. He hadn't found a single thing to criticise in Chivvy Chase School! Like Mr Joe Franks, he thought of returning, but then shrugged his shoulders and drove off for a light lunch. His indigestion seemed to have come back again.

Spiky, when he returned to the classroom, was

deep in thought. During a modelling lesson it was possible to talk, and he was working with Selwyn Jordan, a serious boy who was more used to being ridiculed himself than to poking fun at others. So Spiky decided to risk revealing his thoughts to Selwyn.

'Are you feeling happy, Selwyn?'

'Very,' admitted Selwyn, 'especially as I'm trying to make a model, which I usually hate doing.'

'Everybody looks happy, don't you think?' went on Spiky.

Selwyn took a look around. 'Yes, everybody,' he agreed. 'Including Mr Browser.'

'Everybody's happy inside the school,' mused Spiky. 'Even Lee Franks' dad looked happy when old Sage brought him round.

'That's true,' agreed Selwyn. 'What are you getting at, Spiky?'

'Well, when Mr Franks left the school, he wasn't happy any more. I saw him shake his fist and heard him shout something angrily. Halfway up the path, he was, just like Anna and myself this morning. We were squabbling, and suddenly when we reached a certain point it all stopped and we were as happy as could be. And halfway up the path we passed through something. She felt it just as I did.'

'So did I,' said Selwyn.

'Then you believe me?'

'Of course I do.'

Spiky sighed with relief.

'But not many people will believe it,' Selwyn warned him. 'People won't believe easily in things they can't see.'

'Selwyn,' said Spiky in a confidential whisper, 'I think I know what's happened!'

'Oh, yes?' Selwyn was too polite a boy to laugh his head off at this, and Spiky was grateful.

'Yes. You know when that object of mine began hissing yesterday?'

'Of course I remember.'

'Well, something must have come out of it. I think it must have produced some sort of invisible skin thing, so that everybody inside the skin was happy. Ever since it hissed, we've all been as contented as can be – and for no good reason, really.'

'It could be true,' said Selwyn, frowning. 'I waited for a friend of mine in Mr Caracco's class yesterday afternoon. He was being kept in – but he said afterwards that he had a great time. Caracco played the guitar, and really didn't want to keep them in at all. It all adds up, Spiky!'

'But what can we do? Should we tell Mr Browser?'

'Not yet,' said Selwyn. 'We'll do an experiment first, just to make sure we're right.'

'Experiment?' At first Spiky thought Selwyn was

going to ask about the second, secret object he had at home, and was wondering whether he should admit to having it. But Selwyn had other ideas.

'I go home to dinner today,' he said.

'So what?'

'Well, if we're right, I shall feel different when I leave school and different again when I come back after dinner. I can specially check to see if there really is a change.'

'And if there is?' asked Spiky enthusiastically.

'Then we can tell Mr Browser, and perhaps make him pass through that film thing of yours.'

Spiky had never been more pleased with the usually aloof Selwyn, and he wished him luck when the twelve o'clock bell rang and the few children who went home to lunch left the classroom. Spiky was not worried about the situation, for he was feeling too happy for worry, but he did curiously wonder, if his theory was true, who had made the strange object and why it should act in such a way.

He was even more convinced than ever that there was truth in his idea when Class 8 came out from school dinner.

'Best dinner for a long time,' Michael Fairlie remarked. 'I thought those fish fingers were the greatest.'

'How about the spaghetti bolognaise?' said Anna. 'Better than we had when we were on holiday

46

in Italy.'

'And the cook gave me a second helping,' added Michael. 'She's never done that before.'

Spiky was contentedly full, and the cook was all smiles as she offered other children extra portions. And Mr Sage was standing there beaming happily at everybody. All very jolly, thought Spiky, but there was something very suspicious about everybody being so cheerful at the same time. After lunch he conducted an experiment of his own; he ran to the end of the school field, and just before he reached it something brushed across his face, arms and legs. Had he crossed the other limit of the happiness zone?

He sat by the far railings and watched the happy, peaceful children at play – and now he was out of the magic zone himself, uneasiness began to spread like ink on a piece of blotting paper. Could there be some sinister motive behind all this artificial happiness? He sat down against the railings and waited anxiously for Selwyn to return.

4

Mutiny at Chivvy Chase

Selwyn Jordan returned quickly to school after annoying his mother by devouring his dinner in record time. When he reached the school gate he was anxious and puzzled, because at home he had definitely been in more normal mood – even a little depressed at having to go back to school, and irritated with his mother when she fussed over his food. When he passed through the suspected film halfway up the path, his anxiety and irritation were replaced by a sense of well being and mild curiosity, because now he was aware of the change.

He hurried to find Spiky, and sighted him sitting pensively by the railings at the furthest point from the school. He waved to him to come nearer, but Spiky stayed obstinately where he was and beckoned Selwyn to come to him. When he did so, Selwyn realised why Spiky wouldn't move. As he ran towards him, Selwyn sensed that he had again passed through some invisible barrier, and his concern about the mystery returned.

'Well,' asked Spiky. 'Did you notice anything?'

'You bet I did,' said Selwyn. 'The school's in a sort of happiness belt.'

'And we're outside it here,' added Spiky.

'That's right,' agreed Selwyn. 'I felt myself going through it.'

'Wish I knew what we could do about it,' pondered Spiky. 'They're all so happy in there that they won't want to believe us if we try to tell them there's something wrong.'

'I suppose there is something wrong,' commented Selwyn. 'I mean, if they're all so happy, why not let them stay that way?'

Spiky considered this for a moment, and Selwyn answered his own question before Spiky could put his thoughts into words.

'It's because it's not natural,' declared Selwyn. 'It's the same as people making themselves happy on drugs, or drinking too much. They're usually worse off after a while.'

'That's true,' agreed Spiky. 'And what's more, somebody could have planted that object of mine specially to make everyone happy –'

'So that they wouldn't notice something else happening!' suggested Selwyn.

'Maybe. So we'd better tell Mr Browser about it –'

'No!' said Selwyn sharply. 'If we go inside the happiness area, no one will take any notice of us, and we may not want to make a fuss about it ourselves. We must make them come to us. When the bell rings, we stay here and call the teacher on duty over to us.'

'It's not Browser, it's Caracco,' said Spiky.

'Yes, but if we can persuade more of our class to stay with us, Browser will be told.'

'Anna will come. She knows a bit about my mini-meteorite,' recollected Spiky.

'All right – let's call some of them over,' said Selwyn. 'We've ten minutes to persuade as many of them as we can.'

For the next ten minutes they shouted themselves hoarse and beckoned to as many members of Class 8 as they could see. Anna came across to them first, and Spiky was easily able to explain to her the reasons for the suggested mutiny. With Michael and Martin and other members of the class it was much more difficult. Michael suggested that they'd gone out of their minds.

'All right then,' Spiky challenged him. 'Step three paces back toward the school, and see if you feel anything.'

Michael obeyed – and the expression of mockery on his face vanished. He stepped back again to the railings.

'You're right!' he admitted. 'I feel much better there than I do here.' And he tried the experiment again for a longer time, just to make sure.

Lee Franks was watching them, and suddenly he

joined them.

'Now I know why my dad was so happy in school this morning,' he said. 'The school must be be-witched!'

Then the bell for afternoon school rang.

'Stay here, everyone!' Spiky ordered them. 'We have to make the others see what's happening.'

Mr Caracco appeared and blew his whistle. All the children inside the happy area moved like willing sheep making for their pen – but all those near the railings didn't budge.

'Hurry up, you children!' shouted Mr Caracco. 'I'm not waiting all day for you.'

To his surprise they still didn't move. In normal circumstances there's no doubt that Mr Caracco would have lost his temper, or pretended to do so, and would have rushed up to them and even tried to drag one or two of them away from the railings. But now he was much too contented to register more than curiosity at their unusual behaviour.

'Please, Mr Caracco, fetch Mr Browser,' called out Spiky. 'We'll explain everything when he comes.'

When Mr Caracco smilingly sent off a child to fetch Mr Browser, Selwyn seized on this to con-vince the rest that something odd must be happen-ing at Chivvy Chase.

'They're all under the influence in there,' he

proclaimed. 'Mr Caracco wouldn't normally have sent for Mr Browser – he'd have threatened us with Mr Sage or Miss Toms.'

Nearly all the other children had gone happily into school when Mr Browser appeared on the field and joined Mr Caracco.

'I can't understand what's happening,' Mr Caracco greeted him. 'These children don't seem to want to come into school.'

'What a shame,' said Mr Browser, seeing that most of the mutineers were in his own class. 'I have such a pleasant afternoon arranged for them, too. I'm looking forward to it myself –'

'It isn't that, Mr Browser, honest it isn't,' said Spiky. 'Something funny's happened to the school. It's as though you're all drugged so that you're happy without any real reason.'

Mr Browser recalled his suspicions at the morning assembly, and was thinking about Spiky's statement while Mr Caracco replied to Spiky.

'Then why aren't you all happy too?' he asked, convinced that they wouldn't be able to answer this satisfactorily.

'Because we're beyond the borderline,' Selwyn replied promptly. 'You can feel it for yourselves if you move across here.'

Mr Caracco looked at Mr Browser.

'All right – just to please you,' said Mr Browser,

and he and Mr Caracco took five paces forward and crossed over the happiness border. The children waited expectantly, fearful that maybe the sensation wouldn't work for adults.

'I felt something,' admitted Mr Browser.

'It was like passing through a spider's web,' said Mr Caracco.

'How do you feel, Mr Browser?' called out Anna, and Mr Browser frowned at her.

'I feel most annoyed that you children refused to come in when the bell rang,' he said sternly. 'I'm afraid you'll all have to be punished.'

'That's right,' added Mr Caracco.

'There you are – that proves it!' declared Spiky. 'You didn't say anything about punishing us when you were on the other side, did you?'

'And I bet,' said Lee Franks, 'that if you stepped back again you'd forgive us, just like my dad forgave Mr Caracco this morning.'

Mr Caracco looked a bit surprised, but he had to admit he felt different now that he was standing by the railings.

'I think they're right,' admitted Mr Browser. 'I've been suspicious all day – everyone's been too happy to be true.'

'We'd better tell Mr Sage,' suggested Mr Caracco.

'No, no. Let Mr Sage stay happy,' said Mr

Browser wisely. 'We shall have to try to find out what's going on, and how long it's going to last.'

'Hallo there!' Mr Sage had appeared in the distance on the edge of the field. 'Is everything all right?' he called out.

'Yes, we're just coming, Mr Sage,' Mr Browser called back to him. 'Nothing to worry about.'

'I'm not worried,' replied Mr Sage, and turned and went back into school.

'That proves it,' said Mr Browser. 'He has two classes without teachers in them, and he's still not worried. It's unnatural. If only I knew what was going on!'

'Perhaps I can help you, Mr Browser,' said Spiky. 'Indeed? How?'

'It's that thing I brought into school yesterday – that's the cause of all the trouble.'

Mr Browser looked doubtfully at Spiky. 'We'd better go in now,' he said. 'I'll talk to you about it when we're back in class.'

They all followed the two teachers back across the school field, and once they were inside the happiness zone they wondered what all the fuss had been about. So when they were back in class, there was little interest shown by the rest when Spiky explained to Mr Browser about the strange object and how everyone had been happy since it had hissed.

'Let me have it, Simon,' said Mr Browser. 'I'll take it home with me and try to find out more about it. I have a friend who might help. You haven't any more of them, I suppose?'

It was difficult to lie to Mr Browser, and in the happy classroom atmosphere there seemed to Spiky no reason to hide the truth.

'Yes – I have one more of them at home,' he confessed.

'Look after it,' Mr Browser instructed him. 'It might be very important.' He bent down and, whispering in Spiky's ear, added: 'If I were you I'd bring it in to me first thing in the morning.'

Having given up the shape which he suspected had so much affected the outlook of everyone inside the school, Spiky was prepared to forget all about it and enjoy the rest of the day in the prevailing mood of happiness, but he had reckoned without Anna Cardwell. Classroom conversations rarely pass unheard by third parties, and Anna, who had recently been placed at the front of the classroom by Mr Browser's desk, in order to encourage her to talk a little less, had no difficulty in overhearing most of what Spiky had said. Anna was enjoying Mr Browser's present happy and uncritical frame of mind, and when she heard that Spiky had secretly tucked away another provider of happiness, she decided she must do something about it. During the

57

rest of the afternoon, therefore, she spoke to as many members of the class as she could.

'He's got another one of the meteorite things,' she whispered to her friend Jennifer. 'He hasn't told anyone about it, except Mr Browser. If it can make everyone happy, he oughtn't to be greedy about it. He should bring it to school and be ready to use it, so that if the other one wears out we can all go on being happy. You want to be happy, don't you, Jennifer?'

Jennifer nodded agreement a little doubtfully, because she was normally reasonably happy at school in any case, and didn't land in as much trouble as Anna.

'Well, then, we ought to do something about it,' insisted Anna.

'What can we do?'

'Not much in school – we're all too happy in here to bother much. But after school, when he goes home, we should stop Spiky at the school gate and say we're going to tell about the second meteorite if he doesn't agree to bring it to school and use it here.'

'Yes, but why should he worry if we tell Mr Sage –'

'I didn't mean Mr Sage, silly. I meant the police!'

'The police!' Jennifer was impressed, and so were many other members of the class who had found that easy happiness was much more desirable than being told off and grumbled at nearly every day.

'It's his duty to use it at school,' reasoned Michael Fairlie, 'because he found the things while he was on a school visit.'

This was logical enough for the majority, and Spiky, who had been left to himself during the afternoon, suddenly found himself the centre of interest when he reached the school gate after school.

'Come on, Spiky, own up!' Michael threatened him as they closed around him.

'Own up to what?'

'You know, Spiky. You've hidden another of those mini-meteorites at home!'

'Yes – you're trying to keep all the happiness to yourself. You're being greedy, Spiky,' squeaked Anna excitedly.

'I'm not being greedy!' protested Spiky. 'You don't even know if the thing works. We're only guessing.'

'Come off it, Spiky. You told old Browser about it,' declared Michael.

'That's right, Spiky, and you were pretty sure when you talked to me,' put in Seiwyn.

'Oh, rubbish,' muttered Spiky, and tried to move on – but they wouldn't let him.

'If it's rubbish, bring it in and we'll keep it in school,' suggested Anna. 'Then we can use it whenever we want to if the other one fades out. Just think, on a cold, rainy winter's day when we can't go outside and the teachers are all cross, we could set it going – and we'd all be happy!'

'She's right,' said Martin Portland-Smythe. 'You can't keep a thing like that to yourself, Spiky.'

'Besides, if you try to we shall tell the police about it!' Anna threatened him.

'It's nothing to do with the police,' protested Spiky, but he was shaken by their determination. 'All right – I'll bring it in tomorrow,' he agreed, for the sake of peace.

'You'd better, Spiky!' Michael warned him as the gathering broke up and Spiky was allowed to move off homeward. 'We might as well all be happy together!'

While Spiky was being persuaded to bow to his friends' wishes, Mr Browser was also experiencing the changed atmosphere outside the school as he made his way home. He fingered the curious object in his pocket, and would have liked to dismiss Spiky's ideas as nonsense, but he definitely did feel much less elated now that he was out of the school grounds – more his old, normal self, in fact. Could it be possible that this small, pointed shape could have drugged the school into artificial happiness? He determined to examine it closely when he arrived home. As he walked, he tried to puzzle out

something which was nagging at the back of his
mind – something to do with the search for happiness.

Suddenly he stood still in the middle of the
pavement, right in the path of an old lady carrying a
shopping bag, and snapped his fingers.

'Got it!' he said out loud, and the old lady moved
to one side as if to avoid a madman. 'Professor

McBeagle!' proclaimed Mr Browser – and seeing that he had now attracted the attention of a number of people, turned red in the face and hurried on homeward.

That he should have thought of Professor McBeagle for the first time in at least ten years justified his strange behaviour. Professor McBeagle had been to school with Mr Browser, and then went on to Cambridge University, where he studied biology and psychology, and left with a First, to do work on research in a chemical laboratory. Then, Mr Browser recalled, there came a bad patch in the Professor's life. He had been given a Government grant in order to work on how various foods affect human happiness. He met Mr Browser and told him that he was about to discover a new pill, to be called the Happiness Pill, which would incorporate something of all the foods which contributed most to happiness.

'I'm within a few weeks of completing the formula,' he had assured Mr Browser. 'This pill will change the course of human life on this planet.'

Mr Browser, of course, had congratulated him, and a year went by before he met the Professor again. Now McBeagle was looking thin and drawn, and there was bitterness in his eyes.

'How about the Happiness Pills?' Mr Browser had asked him. McBeagle scowled at him.

'It's all over,' he said. 'The Government wouldn't listen to me. Took away my grant. If you ask me, they don't want people to be happy.'

'I'm sorry about that,' said Mr Browser sympathetically.

'So am I,' said McBeagle angrily. 'But you mark my words, if they won't help me, I'll find someone else who will – somewhere!'

After that meeting Mr Browser had never met the Professor again, though he knew his mother still lived in a house in the area. Surely, thought Mr Browser, the Professor would be just the man to contact about the strange wave of happiness which had descended upon Chivvy Chase. As soon as he arrived home and had greeted his wife, who told him that his car was ready to be picked up at the garage after servicing, Mr Browser searched in the directory for the Professor's mother's phone number.

'Mrs McBeagle here,' came the answer when he dialled the number.

'I don't suppose the Professor is there, by any chance?' asked Mr Browser. 'It's George Browser here.'

'You're in luck,' replied the old lady. 'Bernard doesn't visit me very often these days – he's doing secret work somewhere – but he's here now for a week. Bernard – it's George Browser.'

'Browser?' The Professor's voice was sharp and impatient. 'What can I do for you?'

Mr Browser sensed that he must come quickly to the point.

'I thought you might be able to help me, Bernard. It's about something very odd that's happened at school. Everybody's suddenly become very happy – extraordinarily so, in fact. I remembered you were interested in happiness –'

He was interrupted by the Professor's sudden intake of breath.

'Happiness? In your school? Listen, Browser, have you any idea how this happiness may have started?'

'Yes, perhaps. A boy brought in a strange object from the beach, and suddenly it started hissing, and –'

'That's it!' shouted the Professor, so that poor Mr Browser's ear was temporarily put out of action. 'Where is this thing, Browser?'

'I have it here, Professor.'

'Then hold it, man! For goodness' sake, don't lose it! I'll be round within a few minutes. Stay right where you are!'

The Professor's excitement came over the line so strongly that Mr Browser sat there holding the receiver in his hand, long enough for the Professor to remember that he didn't know exactly where Mr

Browser lived.

'What's your address, man?' he boomed at Mr Browser. 'Ah, yes, I know where that is. Stay where you are! Don't lose that thing, whatever you do!'

Mr Browser put down the receiver and sat there looking at Spiky's object, which he had taken out of his pocket. Why should this strange shape have aroused so much excitement in the Professor? He was still wondering when his wife called him for the fifth time to come and eat, but he hadn't very long to wait before a fierce knocking on the front door made Mrs Browser jump as she was taking her husband's empty plate into the kitchen.

'Who can that be?' she asked.

'An old friend of mine, Professor McBeagle,' Mr Browser told her. 'He's come about a little scientific matter which has cropped up at school.'

He hadn't told his wife about the strange belt of happiness which lay over Chivvy Chase, in case she might not like the idea of him being happier at school than at home.

'You'd think he'd discovered all the secrets of the universe, the way he knocked,' she grumbled, and went into the kitchen.

Mr Browser opened the door, and – 'Browser!' the Professor greeted him breathlessly, stepping inside before he was invited. 'Where's this thing you've found? I must see it – at once!'

65

'It's nice to see you after so many years, Professor,' began Mr Browser politely, but the Professor had no time for politeness. There was a fierce, hard look in his eyes; he was altogether different from the bumbling Professor McBeagle whom Mr Browser had known of old.

'Yes, yes, the object, Browser. Bring it me. I must see it – it's vital!'

'Indeed,' said Mr Browser, who didn't like being hurried. 'Come into my front room, and you shall see it.'

The Professor sprang tigerishly into the room, and waited demandingly there.

'Do sit down, old chap,' Mr Browser begged him, and with an impatient grunt the Professor sat. Mr Browser fumbled in his pocket, and as the Professor's eyes seemed to grow in anticipation, finally produced Spiky's find.

'That's it!' cried the Professor, and grabbed the object like a small child claiming a toy. Swiftly he produced a magnifying glass and inspected one of the pointed ends. 'Yes, yes! It's been discharged!' he cried. 'What an amazing chance! I thought they must all have been lost.'

'Lost? Are there lots more?' asked Mr Browser.

'Yes – dropped in the sea by mistake. Is this the only one you found?'

'I didn't find it,' explained Mr Browser. 'A boy in

66

my class did.'

'And has he others?'

'He told me he has one more.'

'One more! Indeed! Then I must have it.'

'Really?'

'Yes, of course. Browser, you don't seem to realise that the happiness of the whole country, and then of the world may depend on these shapes being found by me and not misused. Nothing must stop my plan to make the whole world happy. Where does this boy live?'

'Spiky – er, Simon Jackson? Not far from here, but I'm not sure of his address, and I couldn't have you calling at his home, Professor. Besides, there's no need. He's promised to bring the thing into school tomorrow morning.'

'Tomorrow morning! That may be too late, if they come to know about it. Nothing must stop me now. You don't understand the urgency of the affair, Browser.'

The teacher in Mr Browser objected to being told he did not understand.

'I might understand, if you would be good enough to explain,' he told Professor McBeagle.

'Browser,' said the Professor, looking at him like a tiger stalking its prey, 'can I trust you? If I explain, will you promise to tell no one, and will you also promise to get the second object from that boy as soon as he enters the school tomorrow, and to hand it to me immediately? I shall be waiting at the school gate.'

'All right,' agreed Mr Browser. 'If it's so important to you, I will.'

'You may recall, Browser, that years ago I was working on a project to produce a happiness pill? Well, I was near to the final solution when the Government took away my grant.'

'I remember. Why did they do it, Professor?'

'Because,' declared the Professor bitterly, 'they didn't want everyone to be happy. They were afraid that if people were too happy, there'd be no need for a Government at all. No need for a police force, no need for an army, no need for politicians to tell people why they were unhappy. So they told me they didn't want any more to do with the pill, even if I did find the solution. You can imagine how I felt! The power to make everyone happy was within my grasp, but these fools wouldn't listen!'

'You must have been upset,' commented Mr Browser, and the Professor gave him a sharp look.

'I was,' he went on. 'But I'm not the sort of man to give up. No, not McBeagle. If they wouldn't help me, I would go elsewhere.'

'Elsewhere? To the Americans, or the Russians?' supposed Mr Browser.

'No, no. They're human as well – they wouldn't

want too much happiness. No, Browser, I decided to look to other worlds. I set up my own radio and astronomical equipment in my own secret laboratory, and I began to probe into space, in the hope of finding beings who would combine with me to bring happiness to their planet and to mine. After several years I made contact!'

The Professor's eyes were afire with enthusiasm, and Mr Browser became uneasy.

'But I understand that all attempts to contact other worlds have so far failed,' he pointed out.

'And they will, they will,' said the Professor, undeterred. 'You see, in order to be in touch with other worlds, you have to be out of touch with your own. That's the factor missing in all these other attempts. The scientists have been too pleased with their own world to be able to listen properly to the signs from space. As soon as I set up the right signal, I received a response.'

'Where from?'

'From a small satellite of Saturn.'

'But I thought –'

'Yes, you thought, like all the rest, that the atmosphere of Saturn and its moons would render life impossible. But on the Secret Satellite, as I call it, the inhabitants are living deep down under a metallic layer which protects them from the upper atmosphere.'

Seeing that Mr Browser looked a trifle disbelieving, the Professor took him by the arm, and held him with his glittering eyes, in the style of the Ancient Mariner.

'You may be sure my friends are there,' he assured him. 'They have been working with me for years on the happiness project. They have discovered a material which contains large amounts of the contents of my happiness pill in the form of invisible gas. This' – pointing to the shape – 'is the kind of container I mean. They sent a first batch of them to me, disguised as meteorites, but by mischance instead of falling on a quiet beach near my home they fell into the sea. I am expecting more soon, and I have my agents set up all over the country. If we can manage to make the British happy, after that the whole world will be easy meat! We shall conquer the world with happiness!'

The Professor swayed on his feet as he contemplated his vision of the future.

'But tell me,' put in Mr Browser gently, 'a rocket has recently been past Saturn, and nothing was said about this satellite with the metallic surface.'

'Of course not,' replied the Professor triumphantly. 'Why do you suppose the camera failed at a certain point when the rocket was passing Saturn? My friends weren't taking any risks. They made sure it jammed at just the right time, so that no suspicions would be aroused.'

'I remember that,' Mr Browser had to admit.

'Mr Browser, there's only one way in which we can be stopped. If the Government finds out, they'll try to produce some kind of anti-happiness formula, and put it in the water supply. First of all, of course, they'll try to collect all the meteorites – that's what they'll call them – and prevent them being used. So they mustn't find out, Browser! The next few days are vital. You want the world to be happy, don't you? Then tell me the address of this boy, will you, and I'll go and collect the other shape.'

71

'I'm awfully sorry, but I can't remember it,' said Mr Browser.

The Professor stood up and clenched his fists.

'Confound it, man, can't we go into school and find it?'

'I haven't the key,' said Mr Browser, 'and Mr Sage, the Headmaster, would be very suspicious if I were to ask for it. No, I'm afraid you'll have to wait until morning, Professor.'

The Professor scowled. 'I can't afford any slip-ups,' he declared. 'Is this boy a healthy specimen? He's not likely to be away from school, I hope?'

'Simon? No, he's seldom away.'

'What does he look like?'

'He's a normal-sized boy, with dark hair and a reddish complexion. His hair stands up at times at the back – that's why the others call him Spiky.'

'Well, I hope Spiky brings that other shape in tomorrow, and I'm sure, Browser, you'll do all you can to further the cause of happiness, won't you? I'm sure such assistance will not be forgotten when we come to power.'

'Come to power?'

Clearly the Professor could happily have bitten off his tongue for allowing that statement to slip out.

'Oh, somebody has to control the degree of happiness and make sure the protective films are renewed where necessary,' he tried to explain.

Mr Browser was by now deeply worried, but he decided not to show his concern.

'Well, Professor, before you go perhaps you'd like to have a drink,' he suggested.

'Just a little one,' the Professor agreed, hoping to disarm Mr Browser of any suspicions he might have. Mr Browser fetched two sherries.

'To happiness,' he toasted, and they drank.

'See you tomorrow morning,' the Professor reminded him as he left. As he walked down the garden path, the Professor's thoughts were only partly on happiness.

'Power is true happiness,' he muttered to himself, and rolled his eyes around in a way he hadn't dared in front of Mr Browser. 'I'll have to get hold of that boy in the morning, come what may!' he told himself, and turned at the garden gate to wave in friendly manner to Mr Browser.

5

Trouble on the Secret Satellite

Imagine what it must be like to live in a world enclosed like a metal box. The inhabitants of the Secret Satellite of Saturn were existing like this, unable to expose themselves to the poisonous gases being blasted along the surface of their world. They had to create their own atmosphere artificially, and they lived in dread of the day when the supplies of chemicals used for this purpose might dry up for ever. They only opened the lid of their world, as it were, when conducting experiments or trying to make contact with other worlds in space.

Little is known so far about them or their world, though according to Professor McBeagle their shape is the same as the mini-meteorites they sent down to earth, and they move around like spinning tops. No doubt they believed that their similarity in shape to the meteorites would help them to invade the earth more easily, for on landing they would at first be mistaken for meteorites.

Imagine their delight when they first contacted Professor McBeagle when he picked up their strange, hissing signals, and indicated to them that he was seeking himself to conquer the world by

means of his happiness formula. In utter frankness they exchanged signals with him, he revealing the extent of his findings, and they the nature of all the substances at their command. Gradually, as they worked together, the Professor's plan for his pill changed, and with the help of a chemical freely available on the Secret Satellite, they turned to the creation instead of huge happiness bubbles. A great amount of highly pressurised gas could be contained in a metallic substance only to be found on the Secret Satellite. The shape best suited to containing the gas was the one described by Spiky as two pyramids fitted together. It was arranged to deliver some small samples to the Professor for testing, just to make sure that the effect on human beings was as expected. After that, bigger and bigger containers, all of the same shape, would be sent, these to be primed to start hissing on landing.

The situation became more urgent for the citizens of the Secret Satellite when they realised that the space probe from the earth was passing close to them. The Professor was able to warn them that the metallic, smooth surface of their world would no doubt attract the attention of worldly scientists, who would be highly interested in the possibility of mining this metallic ball.

Frantically the scientists of the Secret Satellite worked until they had perfected a ray which would

home in on the space probe's camera and temporarily put it out of action while the probe was passing the Secret Satellite. Just in time they succeeded, and as the rocket sped past Saturn and closest to them, its camera mysteriously went out of action, only until such time as it was well out of range of the Secret Satellite. According to the scientists on earth, the camera had jammed and then freed itself – and on earth only Professor McBeagle knew the truth.

Perhaps the excitement and anxiety of the inhabitants after seeing an earth rocket pass close to them, caused them to hurry too much with their preparations, and when they sent off the sample objects, disguised as meteorites, they were a fraction of a degree out in their calculations. Instead of landing on a lonely beach not far from Professor McBeagle's laboratory, where he could easily go out with a metal detector and retrieve them at his leisure, the objects landed on a mudbank off the seaside, and were covered by the sea at high tide.

The Professor secretly called his new allies all sorts of names; by their inefficiency they were threatening his takeover of the world. He spent several days trying to locate the objects, and was about to demand that they make and send some more, when Mr Browser rang him.

The discovery of two of the objects by Spiky threatened the Professor's plans more than Mr Browser knew. The jamming of the space rocket cameras had caused secret speculation amongst scientists, including a rival of McBeagle's, who worked for the Government and was always trying to check on McBeagle, so far without success. But any report of unusual happiness anywhere in Britain could easily lead to a Government investigation. Now the Professor was afraid to ask his friends to send more objects, in case they were detected. His first priority was now to obtain the one Spiky had hidden away, and then to try to discover where the others were lying. Next he wanted to get rid of the happiness bubble surrounding Chivvy Chase School, before Government officials turned up to check on it.

When he returned from visiting Mr Browser he at once sent a delaying message to his collaborators on the Secret Satellite. They were not very pleased about the delay, because they feared lest the passing rocket might have reported their presence through other instruments than the jammed camera. The scene on the satellite was fascinating. The inhabitants lived, rather like hermit crabs, permanently attached to the top-like vehicles which over the years had become part of themselves. Sometimes you can hear people on earth say: 'He's on his bike – or in his car – so often that it's become part of him.' On the Secret Satellite these beautifully balanced spinning tops had really become part of the inhabitants. They lived and slept in them, and only came out of them once in a satellite year so that the vehicles could be serviced. When this happened they lay in hospital beds and were specially looked after, because at that time they were often open to illness.

This was one of the reasons why they were on the lookout for the possibility of living in a healthier climate, where they could perhaps even afford to separate themselves from their top-like vehicles and exist without for ever spinning round and round. The Professor's descriptions of birds and flowers

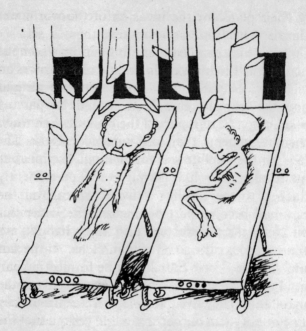

and trees and of the heather on the mountains of his beloved Scotland helped to convince them that earth would be the ideal place for them to begin life anew. They dreamed of being able to look up into a blue sky rather than a metallic, unchanging ceiling; they envied the Professor the feel of rain dripping gently on his face. Most of all they looked forward to the chance of breathing pure, natural air which would gradually make them stronger, healthier and better developed.

Their plans for the invasion of the world were simple. The Professor had sent them a series of signals which enabled them to build up a complete map of the British Isles, including all the towns and villages with their populations. First of all giant diamond shaped containers would be sent off, designed to land in each of the big cities and towns. These were to be activated automatically on landing, which would be in the small hours of the morning.

The balloon-like films would spread out and envelop the cities, and so when the inhabitants woke up they would one and all be happy – even those with tax demands or toothache. At the same time happiness bubbles would be formed in nearly uninhabited areas such as mountains, moors and marshes. These were the areas in which the invaders would land and begin their world conquest. As the humans would still be under the impression that they were ruling themselves, they would be too happy to bother if they detected any signs that in fact the invaders were gradually taking over.

Once the British Isles, a well-known area for grumblers and complainers, a place where it seemed sometimes that people just didn't want to be happy, was rendered harmlessly contented, it would be easy to subjugate the more prosperous European countries. Then the countries in which there was genuine unhappiness would follow with little difficulty.

It was to be a contented world, happy under the rule of the kindly invaders, who would only show a harsher side of their nature if a happiness bubble accidentally burst and the people showed signs of discontent. Professor McBeagle was to be given the position of Chief Adviser for the Happiness of the British Isles, and was to be allowed to continue research work aimed at getting the most out of the happy humans.

Now, Spiky Jackson, by discovering two of their samples, had opened the possibility of investigations being held which could lead to a hostile reception for the invaders. The leading members of the Secret Satellite Invasion Planning Committee buzzed around excitedly on their tops and sent messages hissing out to Professor McBeagle, warning him to take charge of the shapes and destroy the happiness bubble which had formed over Chivvy Chase School too early.

'The boy must be forced to hand over the shape,' the last message warned him. 'If necessary the boy, and anyone else who knows about the shapes, must be silenced. Act fast, Professor, or we may find we need you no longer!'

No wonder the Professor was up and about well before sunrise the next morning, ready to take action in order to maintain his prospects of becoming the most important human in the new regime of Happiness.

6

The Happiness Bubble Bursts

The Professor knew how to remove happiness bubbles as well as how they were to be installed. He arrived outside Chivvy Chase School at five o'clock in the morning, parked his car and climbed over the school gate with his equipment. This consisted of a container full of liquid which was to be squirted at part of the bottom edge of the bubble, and a kind of blow lamp which would then be used to ignite the liquid. Thus a gap would be made through which the gas could pass while the fire slowly ate away at the film so that it could not form up again, as it did when people passed through it.

Having located the film, it took the Professor half-an-hour to go carefully round the bubble, spraying the chemical on to it. Then round he went again, applying his blow lamp. The film burnt away with only very little smoke to show for the fire, and no doubt Professor McBeagle would have been able to creep quietly away had not the school caretaker, Mr Watchett, arrived on the scene. He was early because he was looking forward to another happy day in school. At first he thought he was looking at early morning mist, but then the unusual

smell of the smoke met his nostrils – and he saw the Professor with his blow lamp finishing the job. The caretaker rushed into the school and rang the fire brigade, and by the time he came out again the Professor had run to his car and vanished.

The fire brigade arrived promptly, but by that time all signs of the fire were gone, and the caretaker was sitting in his boiler room looking perplexed.

'I saw this man setting fire to the grass,' he explained, feeling a little stupid. 'I also saw smoke over the school. There was a fire, I swear it.'

'Oh yes,' said the chief fireman mockingly. 'The grass isn't even scorched. What do you suppose the fire was burning? Maybe it was early morning mist you saw. That can be deceiving, especially when you're only half awake early in the morning. Is there nothing else suspicious you have to report?'

'Yes,' said the caretaker sadly. 'The whole atmosphere of the place has changed.'

'Changed? How?'

'I – I don't feel nearly as happy any more,' said the caretaker, and swiftly added, seeing the amazed look on the fireman's face, 'but I don't suppose that matters.'

'I don't suppose it does either,' said the fireman irritably. 'You've had me sliding down a pole at five thirty in the morning, all for nothing. I jolly well hope you aren't too happy.'

So they said farewell and the fire engine drove off, leaving the caretaker brooding over his missing happiness.

'Oh well,' he muttered, 'we had to come back to normal at some time, I suppose. It was too good to last.'

Many children, unusually early at school that day in anticipation of happiness just as the caretaker had been, were disappointed to find that their only feeling on arriving in the school playground was to wish that they hadn't bothered to come so soon. Everything was so obviously normal again – quarrels broke out, small boys were knocked over by big ones without so much as a 'sorry', and girls squabbled or complained they were being left out of games.

Spiky Jackson left home at the usual time, having spent a quiet minute or two in his bedroom trying to decide whether to take the second object with him to school as Mr Browser had requested. Finally he decided not to let Mr Browser down, and slipped the shape into his pocket. Spiky was unhappy at the thought of parting with something which he realised could give him great power. If the first shape had caused the strange happiness in Chivvy Chase School, why shouldn't the second one be used to make his own home a place where he and his family could live happily ever after? He hoped Mr Browser would take a look at the object and then return it to him before the end of the school day.

Spiky hurried towards school, anxious to make sure that the effect of the first mini-meteorite was still working. If the happiness it created only lasted for a short while, then he would do better to hold on to the other one and only use it at a time when it was most needed – perhaps when his mother or father – or both – were about to be angry with him.

He was deep in thoughts like these as he ran along by the gutter, head down and not needing to look ahead on the route to school he knew so well. Suddenly he was awakened to reality by the sound of a car wheel screeching in the gutter alongside him. Startled, he sprang back. The car had been driven from the other side of the road, and a fierce little man with a beard opened the driver's door and beckoned to him.

'You're Spiky Jackson, aren't you?' demanded the fierce little man.

'Yes,' said Spiky. 'How –'

'Never mind how I know. Maybe it's because your hair's up on end at the back. Come here, boy – I've something to ask you.'

Spiky hesitated, then drew nearer.

'Closer, boy – I won't bite you!'

But when Spiky moved a trifle closer, the little man shot out his hand and grabbed Spiky's arm.

'That shape you found, boy – have you brought it with you?'

'Yes,' admitted Spiky in surprise. 'I'm taking it to Mr Browser.'

The little man gave a powerful yank to Spiky's arm, caught hold of him with both hands and dragged him into the car.

'Sit still and be quiet!' he demanded of Spiky, slammed the door and drove off in jerks and shudders.

'But this isn't the way to school!' protested Spiky.

'We're not going to school,' the little man informed him. 'First of all, show me the object you found.'

He drove into a bus lay-by and turned to Spiky to inspect the object in the boy's hand. Grabbing it, the Professor subjected it to a quick inspection with the same magnifying glass he had used on the other one.

'Unused! Excellent!' he muttered. 'Good boy!'

'May I go now?' asked Spiky, holding out his hand as if in the hope of receiving the object back.

'Go? Not likely, my lad. First of all you're coming with me to show me exactly where you found these things.'

'But I found them on a sandbank when the tide was out,' explained Spiky.

'Exactly. The tide is well out this morning. That's

why you're coming with me now.'

'But Mr Browser –'

'Never mind him. You do as I tell you, and you'll come to no harm.'

The Professor put his foot down on the accelerator and the car leaped off in the direction of the beach. Spiky had thoughts of trying to leap from the car, but the Professor's daredevil driving prevented him from risking an escape. The little car shot forward in sudden spurts, screeched round corners and annoyed other traffic all the way to the sea front.

'Tell me where to stop,' the Professor ordered Spiky. 'We're going to try and find some more of those shapes.'

'If we do, may I return to school?' asked Spiky.

'Why not, if you help me,' replied the Professor, but he didn't look at Spiky as he spoke.

'It was near that boat out on the mud,' said Spiky, pointing to the boat which Mr Caracco had told them was to be the limit of their explorations. Professor McBeagle immediately braked hard and pulled into a parking space, then jumped out and ran round to the passenger's door to allow Spiky to come out and at the same time make sure that he didn't try to run away.

'Let's go!' he said. 'Just show me where they are – then you can go back to school.'

Spiky decided to pretend to trust the Professor rather than be dragged unwillingly across the road.

'We'll have to take our shoes off – it's muddy out there,' he advised the Professor.

'No time for that!' replied the Professor, a wild gleam in his eyes. He had hold of Spiky's arm tightly as they rushed across the beach and out on the mud.

'Where are they? Where are they?' he demanded of Spiky as he tugged at his arm. What he said next scared Spiky even more.

'If you don't show me where they are, you'll never go home again, let alone back to school! You'll vanish for ever, Spiky Jackson! If I find them, you can be sure I shall remember you when the Secret Satellite conquers the world!'

'The Secret Satellite?'

'Yes – that's where your mysterious objects have come from,' explained the Professor. 'Now – how much further?'

Spiky didn't like the idea of vanishing for ever, nor did he fancy the world being conquered by some secret satellite, so he slowed down and stood still in the mud, feeling it oozing between his shoes and his socks.

'Was it here?' demanded the Professor. Spiky saw that the tide was beginning to edge over the sand beyond the boat, where the objects, if there were

any more, must be lying. He decided to try delaying tactics.

'It was just near here – not far from the boat,' he lied.

'Show me exactly where you found them!'

Spiky took an instant dislike to the Professor's bullying tone, and decided to risk all and deceive him. He pointed to a muddy patch just on the shore side of the boat.

'Round about there,' he said.

'Show me exactly!' ordered the Professor, and Spiky winced as the little man's fingers dug into his arm.

'It's hard to say,' he grumbled. 'The boat's lying in

a slightly different position – '

'Near as you can! Hurry up, too!'

The Professor, Spiky guessed, was bullying him because he was becoming more and more nervous. He sneaked a look at his watch. It was already five past nine – his presence would be missed at school, though Mr Browser might think he was ill.

'Under the mud here,' he said, taking a step forward and pointing downwards.

'Are you quite sure? I thought Mr Browser mentioned a sandbank?'

'It was near one,' said Spiky. 'Have you met Mr Browser?'

This question made the Professor's temperature rise even higher.

'Confound it, boy!' he said, turning red in the face. 'We've no time for polite conversation now! The happiness of the world could depend on me – and you.'

'It was here,' insisted Spiky. 'The mud was drier that morning. Maybe the tide went further out that day. Mr Browser didn't know exactly where I was – he was sitting on the beach, far away.'

'Why did you start digging about in this mud?' asked the Professor suspiciously as he poked into it with his toes.

'I was looking for crabs,' said Spiky, thinking quickly.

The Professor seemed satisfied, prodded about in the mud a few times with his fingers, then looked back to the shore.

'I can't waste time here,' he told Spiky. 'I'll have to go back to my laboratory and fetch my metal detector along. That will tell me very quickly whether you're telling me the truth or not.'

'There might not be any more,' protested Spiky.

'Oh, yes there are. They sent hundreds.'

'Well, then, may I go back to school now?'

For answer the Professor grabbed his arm again and started walking him towards the shore.

'Not likely, my boy. I can't afford to let you loose. I have enemies who want to stop me making everybody happy. You'll have to come with me to my laboratory, until I've found the other shapes – perhaps until the invasion has taken place.'

'But I can't – '

'Can't? You're going to, my lad. You're my prisoner from now on. And let me tell you, I've a knockout gun handy, like the sort they use on wild animals to keep them quiet. You wouldn't want me to use that, would you?'

Spiky shook his head. When they reached the beach he looked hopefully along the road, but there was no sign of anyone coming to rescue him. The Professor bundled him into his car and drove swiftly away in the opposite direction to the school.

Spiky sat beside him, looking miserable, but the Professor's spirits rose as they drove along.

'I don't know what you're worrying about, Spiky,' he said in a voice much more friendly than before. 'I'm not going to harm you. On the contrary, I'm going to make you very happy. I might as well use the shape you've found, so when we arrive at my laboratory I'll set it off so that both of us are happy – as happy as you were in school yesterday.'

Spiky didn't receive the information with any enthusiasm, so the Professor shrugged his shoulders and concentrated on driving. After a while he burst into song, while Spiky sat, all shrivelled up and frowning, beside him.

'Happy days are here again,' sang the Professor, as they drove out of the town and into the marshy countryside. After a few miles he turned up an unmade road which seemed to be leading to an earthen sea wall. Just before the car reached the wall, the Professor turned off along a path which led between trees to an old house beside the sea wall, the foundations of the building being no doubt under sea level. The car stopped outside the large front door, which had steps leading up to it and two rather battered stone lions, one on either side, guarding the entrance.

'In you go,' said the Professor. 'You can wait in my study – the room on the left.'

He showed Spiky into a large room with book-shelves on each wall, full of books old and new.

'Make yourself at home,' said the Professor cheerfully. 'I'm going into my laboratory just to make sure this thing works.' He took out Spiky's shape and waved it at him. 'You still don't realise how important this is,' he declared. 'I'll set it off, and then I'll go back to the beach to find the rest of them with my detector. Don't be afraid to look at the books. I shall be back by dinner time. I'll not let you starve – and, of course, you'll be absolutely happy, so happy that you won't want to go away.'

'Let me out!' shouted Spiky, and rushed towards the door. The Professor pulled out his gun and shook his head.

'No, my boy. That won't work. You might as well settle back and prepare to be happy. Goodbye!'

He closed the door on Spiky, who heard the key turn in the lock and then the sound of footsteps as the Professor departed. Tears welled up in Spiky's eyes as he stared round the room. The books, he dimly saw, were mostly about space and the planets or about the human body. Spiky stifled a sob. Was the Professor mad? Would he be his prisoner for ever? He went and tried to open the door, and banged on it. All a waste of time; he sat down again – and then he heard a familiar, faint hissing sound. The object was at work!

By the time the Professor had left the house with his super metal detector, Spiky was strolling about the study whistling happily, and absolutely sure that everything would turn out for the best in the end. He was once again in the middle of a happiness bubble.

7

Mr Browser Rides Pillion

Mr Browser was in a nervous, irritable mood when
he arrived at Chivvy Chase School on the morning
after his meeting with Professor McBeagle. He was
irritable because of a sleepless night spent thinking
about the Professor and his claim to represent the
Secret Satellite in its attempt to conquer the world.
He was nervous because first thing in the morning,
even before he had made his wife a cup of tea, he
had decided to telephone his Member of Parlia-
ment and tell him about the Professor and his aims.
He had expected to have difficulty in reaching the
M.P., but to his surprise he was at home. More to
Mr Browser's surprise, he didn't laugh on being told
of Professor McBeagle's plans for the country, but
said he had heard stories about the Professor and
would at once contact MI5. Within minutes Mr
Browser had received a call from a secret agent.

'When the boy Simon Jackson arrives at school,
be sure to obtain the object he is bringing, and keep
it until our men arrive,' the agent warned him. 'On
no account allow the Professor to take the object,
and if possible keep him at the school until he can be
arrested. We have suspected him for a long time of

engaging in treacherous activities – in other words, he's been up to no good.'

So now Mr Browser was hanging about at the school door waiting to see Spiky Jackson enter the playground. He was relieved to feel he wasn't any happier inside the school grounds than out of it, so that things must have returned to normal, but he didn't suspect that Professor McBeagle had been responsible for bursting the happiness bubble. Children kept on passing him and saying 'Good morning' to him, but Spiky was not among them. Mr Sage arrived, carrying his briefcase.

'Morning, George,' he greeted Mr Browser brightly, as if unaware that the happiness bubble had been burst. 'Aren't you coming inside?'

'Just wanted to check on a certain boy,' replied Mr Browser, and the Headmaster shrugged his shoulders and entered the school.

Still Spiky didn't appear, and at last Mr Browser decided he would have to go in and write the date on his classroom blackboard. Mr Sage was very demanding about this. Soon the bell rang, and the children came into school. Gradually the empty seats in Mr Browser's room were filled, until there was only one left empty – the one belonging to Spiky Jackson. Mr Browser called the register, and still Spiky was missing. Mr Browser could remain quiet no longer.

'Has anyone seen Simon this morning?' he asked the class.

'Yes, Mr Browser. I saw him,' said Selwyn Jordan. There were times when Selwyn's polite seriousness could make him annoyingly slow.

'Well – where did you see him?'

'He was talking to a man in a car,' said Selwyn thoughtfully. Mr Browser's concern was clear to see.

'And what happened then?' called out Anna.

'Then he went into the car and the man drove away.'

'Tell me, Selwyn – and this is extremely important – was the man dark haired and did he have a moustache? A short, stocky little man, was he?'

'I couldn't tell if he was short or tall, because he was sitting in the car,' said Selwyn, 'but he did have black hair and a moustache. A fierce sort of man, I'd say.'

'That's the Professor,' said Mr Browser. 'Which way did the car go?'

'In the opposite direction to school – towards the coast,' said Selwyn.

Mr Browser was walking up and down restlessly in front of the class.

'Anna – you saw Simon pick up those objects on the sandbank,' he said, turning suddenly. 'Come with me, will you? The rest of the class – carry on working.'

Anna hurried to the door as the rest of the class tried to decide what was going on before settling to work.

'Has Spiky been kidnapped?' asked Anna as she walked with Mr Browser along the corridor.

'I hope not, Anna.'

'Where are we going, Mr Browser?'

'To see Mr Sage.'

Mr Sage was taking a quick look at the story he was going to read in assembly, when Mr Browser knocked sharply and walked in, leaving Anna outside the door. Mr Sage was surprised to see him.

'This is urgent, Mr Sage,' began Mr Browser in explanation. 'I believe that one of my children has been kidnapped. He's been seen in the car of Professor McBeagle, who is wanted by MI5.'

Mr Sage, who had been thinking about the story of Florence Nightingale, stared at Mr Browser.

'MI5 – Professor McBeagle? This is a school, not a T.V. film studio – '

'But it's true, Mr Sage. Professor McBeagle is in league with some beings from near the planet Saturn, who want to conquer the world by making everybody too happy to notice they've arrived. That's why we were all so happy yesterday. Spiky found some objects they tried to send to Professor McBeagle – that's probably why he's likely to have been kidnapped.'

Mr Sage was tempted to ring the secret bell he had under his desk in case of emergency.

'George – are you all right? Would you like Miss Copewell to give you an aspirin? I'll take your class for a while – '

'No, no. I'm not mad, Mr Sage. You'll soon see that I'm sane. Some men from MI5 are on the way here. Simon was supposed to bring the shape in this morning.'

'Yes, yes, George. Just sit down quietly – '

'Anna Cardwell is outside. She saw Spik – Simon pick up the shapes. Mr Caracco knows about them, too. Shall I bring her in, Mr Sage?'

'All right, then,' agreed Mr Sage, who was afraid that Mr Browser might suddenly attack him if he disagreed with him.

Anna came in and told her story, but Mr Sage was absolutely unwilling to believe it. He was so happy in school every day that he hadn't noticed the difference the happiness bubble had made.

'I think you'll have to go now,' he told Anna. 'Miss Copewell will be ringing the bell for assembly. After that perhaps we can talk again.'

Just then two men strode past the window. A minute later Miss Copewell appeared.

'Two gentlemen to see you, Mr Sage. They say they're from MI5.'

Mr Sage turned pale and Mr Browser and the retreating Anna swam for a few seconds before his eyes. He quickly recovered.

'Show them in,' he said. 'I was expecting them.'

When the two men came in Anna, who had remained just outside the door, thought for the first time how small Mr Sage and Mr Browser were. These men were giant sized, yet had an air of

cleverness about them. They clearly weren't merely all-in wrestlers or heavyweight boxers – they were able to do some quick thinking as well.

'Who's the Headmaster?' asked one of them.

Mr Sage quickly moved back behind his desk. 'I am,' he said.

'We're here on a mission of the utmost importance to the country – and to the world,' said the other one, who had ginger hair and a sandy complexion, whereas his friend had short cropped grey hair, the kind which can make some people look more aggressive and vigorous than younger folk with dark or fair hair. They both produced identity cards from their pockets and held them in front of Mr Sage.

'Oh yes,' said Mr Sage, as though it were natural for them to come to Chivvy Chase School for help if they were in trouble.

'Is this gentleman Mr Browser?'

'It is,' said Mr Sage. 'What can I do for you?'

To his disappointment the men turned their backs on him and faced Mr Browser.

'Anna – you'd better stay,' called out Mr Browser as Anna reluctantly moved off down the corridor at a snail's pace. She came back like a piece of stretched elastic returning to its normal shape.

'The boy Simon Jackson – is he here?' asked ginger hair. 'Has he given you the object he found?'

'I'm afraid he hasn't turned up,' said Mr Browser.

'And Professor McBeagle – where is he?' asked grey hair.

'He's not arrived either. In fact, a boy has just told me that Spiky – er, Simon – was seen entering a car driven by a man whose description very much resembles the Professor's. The car drove away in the opposite direction to the school.'

The men's faces tightened and they looked at each other out of steely eyes.

'He's after the rest!' said one.

'He'll make the boy show where they are,' said the other. 'We must go at once and try to pick the Professor up before he finds them. The boy's life could be at stake. Mr Browser – you know where the objects were found. Come in our car and we'll do our best to catch the Professor.'

'I know roughly where they were found,' agreed Mr Browser, 'but I was dozing on the beach at the time. I couldn't say exactly – '

'Then who does know?' asked grey hair.

'I do,' said Anna. 'I was there when Spiky picked them up. And Mr Caracco knows too. He saw us coming back from the sandbank.'

The men turned suddenly to face Mr Sage again.

'We must have this Mr Caracco too,' declared ginger. 'He must come with us to show us where these children were. Has he transport?'

'Yes – a fast motor-bike,' said Anna.

'Good – he can show us the way. Mr Browser, you can come with us – and we'd better take this little girl too, to find the exact spot for us, if the Professor hasn't already discovered it. Let Mr Caracco come at once, please, Headmaster.'

'But,' protested Mr Sage, 'that means I shall have two classes without teachers – '

'You can do what you like with them,' said grey hair angrily. 'How can you possibly delay when the fate of the world could be at stake?'

'The fate of the world?' repeated Mr Sage, and the man nodded.

'All right, then,' said Mr Sage. 'I'll take the two classes myself, in the school hall.'

He hurried off to fetch Mr Caracco. Mr Browser and Anna went with the men to the car park, where Anna expected to see a Rolls Royce or an Aston Martin standing. She was disappointed. Grey hair stepped forward and unlocked the doors of an ordinary family saloon.

'My dad's car's bigger than that,' said Anna. The men smiled but said nothing. Mr Caracco came running out, very excited and ready to save the world, which was what Mr Sage had told him he had to do.

'Where are we going?' he asked.

'Just keep calm,' ginger hair told him. 'We want

you to drive in front of our car and lead us to the beach, then show us where Spiky Jackson found those objects.'

'Done, man!' said Mr Caracco, sprang on his motor-bike and started it up with a roar.

Mr Browser and Anna sat in the back of the car, which followed Mr Caracco out of the school and on towards the coast. Mr Caracco drove very fast, but the car kept up easily with him and purred along the roads as if wishing it could move faster.

'It's a better engine than my dad's,' admitted Anna, and ginger hair turned and smiled at her.

'It's been specially built for us,' he said. 'The engine can do a hundred and fifty miles an hour if necessary.'

'A hundred and fifty!' said Anna, impressed. 'That's faster than all the speed limits.'

Ginger hair looked as though he might say something else, but his grey haired friend frowned at him sternly. Evidently the car was Top Secret, thought Anna. Mr Caracco drew up on the front just opposite the boat which marked the area where Spiky had discovered the shapes.

'It was just beyond that boat,' explained Anna. 'You'll have to hurry, because the tide's coming up over the sandbank.'

'There's no one out there,' said the driver anxiously. 'Do you suppose the Professor's taken them all already?'

'There's a little man wandering about this side of the boat,' said the passenger. 'He's looking for something.'

'That's the wrong side of the boat,' said Anna. 'He'll find nothing there.'

'Little girl,' said grey hair, 'will you come with us and show us the exact position?'

Anna looked at Mr Browser.

'Just the two of us with her won't arouse suspicion,' said grey hair. We could be her dad and her uncle out to show her a few crabs. And she's the only one who knows exactly where the objects are.'

'All right,' agreed Mr Browser. 'You can go, Anna. Better take your shoes and socks off.'

The men from MI5 did likewise, and then took off their coats and rolled up their trousers. Then they took out a pair of very expensive metal detectors from the boot of the car.

'May I come with you?' asked Mr Caracco.

'No – please wait with Mr Browser in the car. We may need you to take a message for us.'

Mr Caracco clambered into the car and sat beside Mr Browser.

'Messenger boy, eh!' he said glumly. 'What are those two playing at?'

'It is very important,' said Mr Browser, looking out to sea. 'If they can't find those shapes, there could be trouble. I wish I knew where Simon Jackson was, though.'

And he told Mr Caracco all he knew about the shapes and the Professor.

'Jingo!' said Mr Caracco. 'I did feel mighty happy at school yesterday afternoon.'

Mr Browser paid little attention to him. He was following the movements of the little man who had been poking about in the mud on the shore side of the boat. As soon as he had seen the two men coming out with Anna, he had moved away to the right, and was now coming back to shore, not directly but in an arc which was almost a semi-circle, keeping well away from the two men. Gradually he drew near the beach. Mr Browser gripped Mr Caracco's arm.

'That's Professor McBeagle!' he whispered. 'He mustn't see me!'

And Mr Browser ducked down on the back seat in an undignified way, leaving Mr Caracco to stare at him in surprise.

'What's he doing?' asked Mr Browser. 'Keep me posted. I want to know where he's going.'

'He's crossing the road,' said Mr Caracco. 'He has one of those metal detector things in his hand.'

'Yes, yes, that would be him!'

'He's going in the direction of a little car – a red one. He's reached it. He's getting into it!'

'Caracco – we musn't lose him! He must know where Simon Jackson is.'

'Shall we tell the others?'

'No,' decided Mr Browser. 'They want to save the country, and so do I, but I also want to save Spiky Jackson. Caracco, we must follow him!'

'Are you going to drive?' asked Mr Caracco

enthusiastically. He imagined himself driving the powerful car and overtaking the Professor, forcing his car into a ditch and then overpowering him with a special grip he'd learned at judo. Playing the guitar at Chivvy Chase School was not enough to satisfy the athletic Mr Caracco completely.

'No, no, Caracco. We can't take a car belonging to MI5,' declared Mr Browser, sitting up a little to spy on the Professor, who was now seated in his car.

'Why, then, we'll go on my motor-bike!' said Mr Caracco, even better pleased at this thought.

'But how shall I come?' asked Mr Browser.

'On the pillion, of course. It'll be child's play to corner him,' declared Mr Caracco, rubbing his hands together in anticipation.

'On the pillion?' Mr Browser looked worried. 'I haven't been on a motor-bike for thirty years. I'll fall off!'

'No, you won't. All you have to do is to hang on to me.'

'Confound it – he's starting,' said Mr Browser. 'He's put his indicator out. All right – I'll come with you, for the sake of Simon Jackson. But do be careful when you go round corners.'

They hurried from the car and Mr Browser was put in position on the back of Mr Caracco's bike. The Professor's red car was already a couple of hundred metres away along the front.

111

'Hold on!' shouted Mr Caracco, and Mr Browser grabbed him so hard around the waist that he gasped for breath.

'Not so tight!' he gasped, and started up his bike with such a roar that it was Mr Browser's turn almost to fall off from fright.

'Hurry up!' he yelled into Mr Caracco's ear. 'We'll lose him if we don't move quickly.'

'No worries,' replied Mr Caracco. 'We're on our way – don't let go!'

Mr Browser hung on for his life as Mr Caracco accelerated along the front as if he thought he was playing a part in a super spy film. Towards the end of the promenade the road led them out into the countryside, and a friendly set of traffic lights allowed them to see the Professor's car waiting ahead of them. Once on the country roads, Mr Caracco had no difficulty in tailing the Professor, who seemed not to be aware that he was being chased.

'Now I can take him!' shouted Mr Caracco. 'Shall I force him into the hedge?'

'No, no, Caracco!' yelled Mr Browser. 'We want to find Simon, not capture the Professor. Just keep on following him and he'll maybe lead us to Simon.'

Mr Caracco was very disappointed, but he obeyed Mr Browser, and dropped back a little, keeping Professor McBeagle's car well in view all the time. Mr Browser was just beginning to be used to the roarings and swervings of Mr Caracco's bike when the Professor turned into the little lane by the sea wall.

'Stop!' ordered Mr Browser. 'It's not far to the house – we'd better follow on foot.'

So Mr Caracco put his bike by the hedge and they walked in single file down the lane, Mr Browser leading. The Professor got out of his car and approached the front door of the house.

'Shouldn't we rush him now?' asked Mr Caracco eagerly. 'I could get him down in a few seconds. Suppose he goes inside and locks us out?'

'Wait,' said Mr Browser, stopping suddenly.

'Look what he's doing!'

The Professor had stopped too, and took something out of his pocket.

'It's a little box,' whispered Mr Caracco. 'He's taking something out of it – and he's put it into his mouth.'

'Yes, of course. A pill,' said Mr Browser. The Professor walked on and stood in the doorway.

'How do you know it was a pill?' asked Mr Caracco.

'I'm guessing,' admitted Mr Browser, 'but I'm pretty sure it was an anti-happiness pill. He must have used the second object Simon found, and now Simon is trapped in a happiness bubble. He won't want to escape – he's a willing prisoner – and the Professor wants to make sure he doesn't give way to happiness too soon himself.'

At this point the Professor turned round. Then he opened the door and entered the house.

'Do you think he's seen us?' asked Mr Caracco.

'Don't know,' replied Mr Browser. 'He probably thinks he's safe enough inside the happiness bubble. He could easily persuade anyone who tried to break in to rescue Simon that it would be much more sensible to work for general happiness – '

'But he doesn't seem to want to be happy himself.'

'Not yet. He knows that if he's going to help in the conquest of this country, then he can't afford to be too contented himself. People who try to conquer others are never happy and contented. Look at Hitler and Napoleon and Alexander the Great. Were they happy?'

'No,' said Mr Caracco, looking at Mr Browser with increased respect. 'But in that case, how are we going to rescue Simon? If we go inside, we'll be happy too, and we may not want to bother to bring Simon out.'

'That could be,' agreed Mr Browser. 'We have to promise each other to force the Professor to hand over his anti-happiness pills, then we could carry on with the rescue after we'd taken a pill each.'

Their problem took a new turn when suddenly the front door was flung open and the Professor appeared, pushing Spiky Jackson in front of him. The Professor looked angry and threatening, while Spiky was allowing himself to be pushed along like an amiable sheep. Mr Browser and Mr Caracco dodged into the shelter of the uneven hedge.

'I know what's happening,' guessed Mr Browser. 'The Professor's taking Simon back to the beach, and he's going to force him to show where the fallen objects really are. He must still be hoping to find them.'

'What must we do?' asked Mr Caracco.

'This time we must stop him,' decided Mr Browser. 'If he returns to the beach and sees that our men and Anna have already removed most of the objects, he may try to kidnap Simon for good. If we hide as they drive past, can you overtake him on a country road?'

'I'll try,' said Mr Caracco. 'We'll have to run back to my bike as quickly as we can after the Professor's gone by.'

They forced their way through a gap in the hedge, and waited until the little red car hurried down the lane. Now that he was outside the happiness bubble, Spiky looked drawn and anxious. As soon as they had passed by, Mr Caracco and Mr Browser thrust themselves back on the lane and ran towards the motor-bike. Mr Caracco had started it up before Mr Browser had arrived, puffing and panting.

'Cling on tight,' Mr Caracco warned him with a gleam in his eyes. 'I'm going to give her all I've got.'

Mr Browser shut his eyes as Mr Caracco opened the throttle and hurtled them through the countryside as if he were in a T.T. race. Ten minutes past, and there was no sign of the Professor in front. Mr Browser was worried. Could he after all have turned off in some other direction than the coast? Mr Caracco roared round corners even faster, and when Mr Browser opened his mouth to protest, the rush of air into it silenced him.

'There he is!' cried Mr Caracco. 'Don't let go!' He

then made a final hair-raising spurt which took him past the surprised Professor at a point where no sane driver would have overtaken. Mr Caracco slowed down and waved the Professor to park at the side of the road. When the Professor refused, and even tried to accelerate past him, Mr Caracco slowed down even more until the bike was wobbling from side to side and Mr Browser feared he would fall off at any moment. Spiky's earnest face could be seen as he watched the antics of his teachers from the passenger seat.

At length the Professor gave up and pulled into the hedge. Mr Caracco at once did likewise and jumped off his bike, leaving it and Mr Browser to topple to one side. Then the Professor made his big mistake. He jumped out of his car and ran towards Mr Caracco, waving his arms in protest.

'Get out of my way!' he shouted. 'I'm on a most important mission!'

'And so are we!' retorted Mr Caracco calmly.

'You – what are you doing?' asked the Professor in surprise. Then he recognised Mr Browser, who had just crept out from under the motor-bike.

'Our mission is to stop you!' declared Mr Caracco, and before the Professor could turn to run he had sprung at him and laid him low with an expert judo movement. Mr Browser hurried to join them. By the time he arrived Mr Caracco was kneeling

with one knee on the Professor's back, and with
both arms was pulling the Professor's right arm
round behind him.

'Let me go!' begged the Professor. 'I have to take
this boy back to school –'

'We know where you're going with this boy,' said
Mr Browser. 'What you intend to do with him
afterwards I don't know, but I can't imagine you
would be taking him back to school. No – he knows

too much for that!'

Mr Caracco tugged at the Professor's arm a little, and the Professor groaned.

'You wanted to conquer the world,' said Mr Browser, 'but your plan has failed. MI5 and Anna Cardwell are on the beach now, looking for the rest of those mini-meteorites.'

The Professor groaned again.

'Do you still want to conquer the world?' demanded Mr Browser.

'I'm – I'm not sure,' said the Professor, and Mr Caracco sat on him harder.

'You still fancy conquering the world?'

'No,' said the Professor. 'I want you to get off my back.'

Spiky had now joined them, and was staring at the athletic Mr Caracco with great admiration.

'I'll let you go,' said Mr Caracco, 'if you'll promise to drive Mr Browser and Simon back to the beach and then hand yourself over to MI5. I shall be riding in front of you, and if you try any funny tricks I shall soon have you on the ground again – and I'll tell the Secret Service you've tried to escape.'

'There's no way out, McBeagle,' said Mr Browser. 'You can still save yourself by owning up, and if you do we won't say much about the kidnapping of Simon here. We'll just say you wanted him to show you where the objects were. Why not help your own country instead of some satellite of Saturn?'

With Mr Caracco's knee still pressing into his back, it was easy for the Professor to see the sense in what Mr Browser was saying.

'I agree,' he said. 'Please get off my back.'

Mr Caracco stood up, and Professor McBeagle picked himself up gingerly.

'Are you a member of the Secret Service?' he asked Mr Caracco respectfully.

'No,' replied Mr Caracco a little sadly. 'I'm just a teacher at Chivvy Chase School. Now get into the car with Simon and Mr Browser, and we'll head back for the beach.'

Gloomily the Professor took the wheel and followed Mr Caracco all the way back to the promenade.

'You're all right, Simon, I hope?' was all Mr Browser said on the journey.

'Yes, thanks, Mr Browser,' said Spiky, and then all three were silent, wondering what would happen when they arrived back at the beach.

The car belonging to the two MI5 men was standing where it had been parked, and Anna and the two men could be seen coming back across the mud. One of them was now carrying a large plastic bag in his hand. They reached the beach and climbed up some wooden steps to the promenade

– and then Anna saw Mr Caracco leaning against the door of the Professor's car.

'Mr Caracco!' she called out. 'We found them!'

The two men came across, and Mr Caracco stood aside to allow them to see Spiky, Mr Browser, and most important of all, the Professor.

'So – you are here, McBeagle!' said grey hair.

'Yes, thanks to these three people,' said the Professor glumly. 'And but for this boy' – he pointed to Spiky – 'I might have conquered the world!'

'We'd like to hear more about that,' said grey hair. 'Kindly step out of your car and into ours, Professor, and consider yourself under arrest.'

The Professor obeyed them instantly.

'Thank you very much, you gentlemen, and you children,' went on the MI5 man. 'We're very grateful, and no doubt you'll be hearing more from us. We'll take you back and drop you at the school before we return to London with this gentleman.'

'Coming, Mr Browser?' asked Mr Caracco, moving towards his motor-bike.

'No thanks,' said Mr Browser.

'I'll go with Mr Caracco,' said Spiky. 'I've ridden pillion before.'

'All right,' agreed Mr Browser, relieved, and they all returned to Chivvy Chase School, where Mr Sage was delighted to see them, and hastened to return them to their classrooms. As Spiky and

Anna went to their places, Anna grinned widely and winked at Spiky several times.

'What's the matter with you?' asked Spiky. 'Why are you looking so pleased with yourself?'

'Wouldn't you like to know!' was all that Anna would reply, and she was still smiling happily as she sat down in her place.

8

The Last of the Mini-Meteorites

When the gentlemen from MI5 had departed, Mr Sage had, of course, to be told exactly what had happened. On hearing Spiky's story and the details of how he was rescued, the Headmaster was convinced that in a very short time his school would hit the headlines and that he would have to appear on T.V. to explain to the public how it came about that Chivvy Chase had played such a large part in saving the world from the effects of the mini-meteorites. He was hopeful, too, that at a later date he would be awarded an M.B.E. from a grateful monarch.

At first Spiky, too, was hoping that an official fuss would soon be made of him. All that happened was that his parents received a letter from London to express the regret of the Government that their son had become mixed up with the eccentric Professor, and trusting that his adventure had caused no ill effects to Spiky. As he hadn't told his parents much about what had happened, this letter only caused much confusion.

'What's all this nonsense about a mad Professor?' demanded Spiky's dad. 'Why didn't you give him that meteorite thing, instead of letting him take you away?'

'Yes – you know we've always told you not to go with strange men,' put in his mother.

'But Mum, he dragged me in – '

'You shouldn't have gone so near to him!'

After a while Spiky began to wish he were back in a happiness bubble rather than having to answer these questions, which turned the whole amazing adventure into a boring defence of his own behaviour. So he kept quiet at home. At school he found life even more unsatisfactory.

'When are they going to knight you, Spiky?' Michael Fairlie would demand at least once every day. 'Why are they so long about it? Could it be that they don't believe you? Maybe they're right. Maybe you made it all up!'

'You're just jealous. You saw the mini-meteorite,' Spiky would reply grumpily. As the days passed he thought less and less about the affair, and even Michael forgot to ask his mocking questions. Mr Sage, too, lost hope that Chivvy Chase School would ever become famous.

The truth was that an affair such as the one Spiky had been involved in becomes Top Secret as soon as certain important people in London find out about it. Mr Sage and Spiky were both doomed to disappointment; they would never hear anything more about the meteorites or the Secret Satellite or

Professor McBeagle – unless events forced them to do so.

Only one person, years later, heard what happened to the Professor, and that was Mr Browser, who met him out shopping one day in a town some miles away. To his surprise, he learned that the Professor had not been put in prison for trying to conquer the world.

'Oh no, it doesn't work like that,' said the Professor, laughing. 'I saw the game was up, so I promised to help the Government. I'm assisting them to make anti-happiness pills, enough for all the population, just in case the Secret Satellite people try to invade us after all. We're keeping a constant watch for meteorites, and as soon as there's a red alert a dose of anti-happiness pills will be put in the water in the reservoirs. Also, a sharp watch is being kept to make sure that no particular section of the people suddenly becomes unusually happy. That would be most suspicious. Me? As for me, I'm allowed to live in my happiness bubble as long as I promise to work for the Government. It's all turned out very well, considering.'

So far it's pretty clear that no attempt has been made to infiltrate the world by means of artificial meteorites. The Government makes sure now and again that the people are not too happy by raising the taxes and the price of petrol and sweets, but the anti-happiness pills are stored up ready for use in some secret Government warehouse. Attempts to contact the Secret Satellite of Saturn have failed – the hissing sounds which come in from space are intelligible to no one, not even the Professor, now that he's in tune with his own world again.

Yet there is somebody, apart from a few very high-up officials in the Government and MI5, who still possesses evidence that the happiness bubbles really did exist. Selwyn Jordan of Class 8 knows who it is, because he overheard a conversation between Spiky Jackson and Anna Cardwell, which went like this:

'Do you think those secret agents found all those meteorite things?' asked Spiky.

'I should think so – most of them,' replied Anna.

'Only most of them? Why do you say that?'

'They picked up all they could find with their metal detectors, and I heard one of them say that some more men would be sent at the next low tide to make sure they hadn't missed any.'

'Well, then, they've taken them all by now,' suggested Spiky.

'Not quite!' Anna grinned at him. 'You see, I saw one of the mini-meteorites fall out of the plastic bag the grey haired man was carrying. He thought he'd put it inside, but it stuck in a fold near the top of the bag and fell out on the sand. While they were looking for more, I picked it up and pushed it behind the ribbon I tie up my hair with at the back. I was afraid all the way back to school that it might drop out, or that one of them might see it – but I was lucky!'

'So you've got one!' said Spiky, annoyed to think that he'd lost the two he'd found. 'Where is it?'

'At home,' said Anna. 'I didn't mean to tell anyone about it. You won't give me away, will you, Spiky?'

Spiky thought for a little, but Anna had put on one of those looks of appealing innocence which could soften the heart of any teacher, and Spiky was quickly conquered. He shook his head.

'Course I won't give you away,' he said. 'What are you going to do with it, though?'

'First of all,' said Anna thoughtfully, 'I had the idea of bringing it to school and using it on a rainy day when Mr Browser is in a bad mood. But those men might come back if they found out there was another happiness bubble at the school. I might set it off one day at home, when my baby brother's yelling and my mum is tired out and makes me stay in and do the washing up. But on the other hand,' she concluded, smiling as she looked into the future, 'I might wait until I have kids of my own and they start playing me up. Yes, I reckon grown-ups can do with a happiness bubble more than children.

I'm pretty happy most of the time anyway. Aren't you, Spiky?'

'Suppose so,' admitted Spiky after consideration. 'I hope it works for you, Anna, whenever you make use of it.'

'Thanks,' said Anna. 'I'll let you know if I use it soon.'

'Would you let me drop in sometimes?' asked Spiky.

'Maybe,' said Anna dreamily, but she wasn't really thinking about Spiky. 'I'd like to think I could live happily ever after.'

'So would I!' declared Spiky.

Who knows – maybe they did!